'Have you ev[...]

He didn't want to [...]
to talk about he[...] [...] [...] out
everything.

'No,' Bryce answered. 'I've never found the right girl.'

'Really?' Her deep blue eyes widened. 'I find that difficult to understand.'

Did that mean she was interested in him despite her apparent indifference? He felt a sudden hormonal surge. And then berated himself because he knew nothing about her. For all he knew she could be the same as the rest. 'It's not because I've been short of choice,' he said. 'There's simply been none whom I've wished to marry.'

'You have very exacting standards, is that it?' she asked, her fine eyebrow delicately arched.

'I suppose so.'

'And you've never found Miss Perfect?'

'Not yet.' But maybe today he'd got lucky.

Born in the industrial heart of England, **Margaret Mayo** now lives in a Staffordshire countryside village. She became a writer by accident, after attempting to write a short story when she was almost forty, and now writing is one of the most enjoyable parts of her life. She combines her hobby of photography with her research.

Recent titles by the same author:

THE WIFE SEDUCTION

HER WEALTHY
HUSBAND

BY
MARGARET MAYO

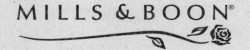
MILLS & BOON®

For Sheila and Hank
With happy memories of a wonderful holiday

First published in Great Britain 2001
Harlequin Mills & Boon Limited,
Eton House, 18-24 Paradise Road, Richmond, Surrey TW9 1SR

© Margaret Mayo 2001

ISBN 0 263 82560 4

Set in Times Roman 10½ on 12½ pt.
01-1201-47593

Printed and bound in Spain
by Litografía Rosés, S.A., Barcelona

CHAPTER ONE

HE HAD the most compelling eyes Lara had ever seen— an unusual smoky grey, almost blue and yet not quite. They were the best part of his face, lashes long and thick, matching the raven blackness of his hair. His attention had immediately focussed on her and maybe she should have felt flattered, most women would, but instead it gave her an uncomfortable feeling.

She turned to her aunt, found that she was watching this man watching her, a faint, approving smile on her lips. It was Helen's Welcome to Australia party. 'You need to get to know people,' she'd said, and against Lara's wishes had invited half the neighbourhood.

'That's Bryce Kellerman.' Her aunt turned and looked at her. 'Come, let me introduce you.' And before Lara could demur she'd taken hold of her arm.

The grey eyes never wavered as they approached. The man eased himself away from the veranda rail, straightened his back, and waited. He was casually dressed in beige moleskins and a brown open-necked shirt that hid none of his tightly muscled body. A deep tan suggested he worked outdoors most of the time.

And he was tall.

Lara hadn't realised quite how tall until she stood in front of him. She was five-nine and he towered over her. Six-four she guessed, at least. Six feet four inches of raw, male animal. Not particularly handsome, a slightly hooked nose and a strong square jaw, and a straight mouth that needed to be more generous. It was the eyes that had it. Close up she could see the dark outline that defined them, the unusual mixture of blue and grey, and the almost brazen confidence that he could fell with one swoop any woman he set his sights on.

And she was in the firing line!

'Lara, I'd like you to meet Bryce Kellerman, long-time friend and jack of all trades. I don't know what I'd do without him. Bryce, this is my niece, Lara Lennox.'

'Good to meet you, Lara.' Grey eyes locked into hers as he extended his hand, reading her soul, instantly knowing everything about her. Lara looked away.

She glanced down at their hands instead. Hers looked pale by comparison. His fingers were square-tipped, nails neatly manicured; he had broad hands, strong hands, more used to manual labour than caressing a woman. The thought horrified her the instant it was born and she snatched away.

He gave a faint, knowing smile, as if well aware of her thoughts. As if! No man could possibly know what another person was thinking. Nevertheless it was the impression he gave. He was a woman's man without a doubt.

But not this woman! He didn't interest her, no man did. She'd had enough pain to last her a lifetime. Her own fault, admittedly, but it was a mistake she didn't intend repeating. And if her aunt had it in mind to do some matchmaking she was deeply mistaken.

'I'll leave you two to get acquainted.' Helen smiled widely and happily. She was in her early fifties, slim, blonde, looked about forty, had been a widow for ten years, and Lara couldn't understand why some other man hadn't snapped her up.

Lara had been six when Helen emigrated from England seventeen years ago and her aunt hadn't been home since, not even when her husband died. She had no children but had many friends and loved Sydney so much that she said she'd never move away. But she'd always kept in touch with her sister, phoning almost every week, and when Helen had heard that Lara's marriage had unhappily ended she'd immediately invited her to stay with her for as long as she liked. She'd even sent money for the plane ticket.

'So, how are you enjoying Australia?'

Bryce Kellerman's voice was so deep that it vibrated through Lara's bones. It was as though her body was the string of a guitar and he'd plucked it. Feeling this man's dynamic sexuality was something she hadn't expected and didn't want. Escape was uppermost in her mind.

'Very much,' she said with a reluctant smile, 'although I've hardly had time to form a proper opinion.'

'The heat's not too much for you?' He was leaning back against the veranda rail now, relaxed and utterly sure of himself, one brown-booted foot crossed over the other, thumbs hooked into a wide leather belt. 'You'll need to take care.'

Lara nodded. 'I'm doing that.' Because of her fair skin she ladled on lashings of sun screen whenever she went out and always wore a wide-brimmed hat. It was something her aunt had instilled into her the moment she'd arrived.

'English roses, that's what your skin reminds me of.'

'I bet you say that to all the girls,' she retorted sharply.

Such compliments annoyed her. They were so glib, so practised; Roger had been a past master at it.

'Only if it happens to be true—which it is in your case,' he said softly, brushing the back of one finger across her cheek. A gentle touch and yet Lara felt as though he was branding her and she turned her head swiftly away.

'You don't like me touching you?' He sounded as though he wasn't used to this sort of reaction.

'No, I don't, as a matter of fact.' Lara held his gaze, ignoring her quickened heartbeats.

'I'll try to remember that.' But it didn't sound as though he was going to make much of an effort. 'Do you know that you look remarkably like your aunt?'

'More like her than my mother actually,' she agreed. 'They're sisters.'

'The same blonde hair, the same wide-spaced blue eyes. Your mouth is a little more—generous.' He smiled. 'I was going to say kissable but something tells me you wouldn't like that?'

'You're learning.'

'What's put you off men?'

'Who says I'm off them?' Her shoulders stiffened automatically. He was too perceptive by far.

Well-shaped dark brows rose and disappeared into the thatch of hair that fell across his brow. 'You're giving a very good performance of not liking them. Unless it's me you resent? Am I missing something? Have you heard something bad about me?'

'I didn't even know you existed until a few seconds ago,' she answered tartly, and he'd have done her a favour if he hadn't turned up. There was something about Bryce Kellerman that Lara instinctively distrusted. She felt that he was the sort of man who would use women for his own purpose and then toss them to one side without a thought for their feelings.

The way he'd deliberately set his sights on her proved it. She was a newcomer, she was blonde and good-looking—she'd been told that enough times even though her mirror suggested otherwise. Her brow was too high, her eyes too big, her mouth too wide, and compliments that she knew were untrue didn't please her.

'And now that you know I exist?' Brows rose laconically, smoky eyes showed dangerous interest.

'I think I'll steer clear,' she answered decisively, and looked deliberately away. 'There's someone else I want to speak to. If you'll excuse me...'

But Bryce Kellerman was not ready to let her go. 'I haven't finished with you yet.'

Lara frowned meaningfully down at his hand on her arm and then looked straight into his face, not speaking until he let her go. 'Thank you,' she said with exaggerated politeness. 'What do you mean, not finished? I wasn't aware that we'd started anything.'

'Helen wants us to become friends.' His smile was slow and confident. 'It would be rude to disappoint her.'

It was Lara's turn to lift her brows. 'My aunt can want all she likes. I choose my own friends. She had no right discussing me.'

'She didn't.'

'Then, how—?'

'Your aunt is of the opinion that it's time I found myself a wife.'

'And I somehow suspect that she thinks I should find another husband,' added Lara wryly.

All of a sudden they both burst out laughing.

'I think we should at least pretend that we like each other,' said Bryce in a wickedly loud whisper.

'It will make Helen's night,' she agreed.

'We don't have to go on with it afterwards.'

'Just for tonight?'

Bryce nodded. 'Shall we take a walk in the garden?' He held out his hand and after a second's hesitation Lara slipped hers into it. Glancing back towards the house she saw Helen watching them, saw her aunt give a nod of approval, and after that they were out of sight. They were two souls together in the blackness of the night. They could hear the music and voices and laughter but could see no one, and no one could see them.

Without warning Bryce took her into his arms, and to Lara's horror she felt an immediate response. Since the breakdown of her marriage she'd avoided men like the plague, so why this sudden reaction? Why this tingling in her limbs? Why were her pulses pounding? It had to be because she felt flattered. What woman wouldn't feel a stirring of her senses when a man as magnetic as Bryce Kellerman sought her out?

But he was mistaken if he thought she would let him kiss her. It might be a magical, moonlit night. It might be warm, sensually warm, an evening made for love, but it was not for her. 'Is this a typical Australian greeting?' she asked, wrenching free. 'I hadn't realised I was supposed to fall into the arms of every man I met.'

'My apologies.' He gave a curt little nod. 'Why don't we sit down and you can tell me about this guy who's ruined your life?' He steered her towards a bench a few feet away.

'I thought you said my aunt hadn't told tales,' she retorted sharply.

His broad shoulders lifted. 'Helen is the soul of discretion. It's nothing more than a calculated guess, but an accurate one judging by your reaction. He can't be much of a man to let go a beautiful woman like you.'

More flattery! Lara felt like kicking him. 'As a matter of fact, *I* left him,' she informed Bryce tightly. Far below, on the opposite bank of the river, house lights twinkled like giant stars. The sky was a deep midnight purple, there was hardly a sound except for the murmur of voices coming from the veranda. It was an idyllic spot and she didn't want this man messing up her mind with talk about Roger.

'How long were you married?'

'Three years.'

'What was he like?'

Lara gave him a hard stare. 'What's it to do with you?'

'It's therapeutic to talk about your problems.'

Her eyes flashed. 'I don't have a problem. Except that you're being a nuisance asking questions I don't want to answer.'

A faint smile softened the hard lines of his face, made him look more understanding and approachable. 'That's the trouble, Lara, you're bottling up your hurt. It does help to talk. How long's it been since your divorce?

'Nearly four months.'

'So the wound's still raw?'

Lara nodded. She didn't look at him, didn't want to see any compassion in his eyes; she was thinking back to the day she'd declared to her school friends that it was her ambition to marry a rich man.

The youngest of five children, brought up by a single

parent, Lara had sworn that she was never going to get into that same situation. She had known what poverty was like, how her mother had struggled to make ends meets. It wasn't for her.

She'd stayed on at school to get her A levels then had found a job with a PR company, and it was here that she had set her sights on Roger Lennox.

Roger had owned the company. He'd had pots of money and wasn't bad-looking either. The trouble was, he'd known it. He'd had every nubile female employee drooling over him, and he'd lapped it up. Lara had known that she would have to do something outstanding to make him notice her.

Her opportunity had come one day when she'd been crossing the car park and had seen her employer sitting in his low-slung silver convertible. 'Goodnight, Mr Lennox,' she called cheerfully.

'Oh, er, goodnight.' He looked up abstractedly. His car, for some reason, didn't want to start. He was both embarrassed and angry—and so would she have been if she'd bought such an expensive car and it failed her.

She turned back to him. 'Can I help?'

Roger had blond hair and blue eyes and was slightly overweight, but his charm made people forget it. He was like a Greek god, some of the girls claimed. Those blue eyes looked at her now scornfully. 'You're a woman.'

'It doesn't mean I don't know anything about engines.' Lara tossed back. Being the only girl in a family of boys she had spent a good part of her life watching them pull cars apart and put them back together, helping whenever they'd let her. She knew as much as any man about the way a car's engine worked.

Roger Lennox frowned. 'Are you serious?'

'Of course I am. Open your bonnet.' She didn't dare to think that he would, but amazingly he did as she asked, although his frown deepened and she could see that he wasn't sure it was wise.

And when he got out to inspect what she was doing, when one thigh brushed against hers, Lara felt the full impact of his sexuality. It was what every girl in the building fantasised over. 'You sure you know what you're doing?' he asked.

'I wouldn't have offered if I didn't.' She tried to sound nonchalant but it was difficult. He *was* attractive without a doubt, and he did quicken her heartbeats, but more importantly he was part of her strategy and her hands trembled as she checked that everything was as it should be. 'Would you like to try it again?' she asked huskily, mentally crossing her fingers that it would start. She wanted to make an impression, not a fool of herself.

The engine sprang into life at the first turn of the key. Roger Lennox looked at her disbelievingly as she appeared from behind the bonnet. 'What did you do?' It was clear he had never tinkered with a car engine in his life.

Lara shrugged. 'The distributor lead had worked loose.'

'I'm impressed. I didn't know women knew about these things. Let me give you a lift home, it's the least I can do.'

Triumph welled in her. She couldn't have orchestrated this any better if she'd tried. She dropped the bonnet, wiped her hands on a tissue, and slid into the seat beside him.

'Where are you?' Bryce Kellerman's deep voice broke into her thoughts.

Sitting beside another man. Ruining my life.

Roger Lennox had sent her flowers the next day, causing a furore in the office. It had been good manners, or so she told herself, to go and thank him. One thing had led to another. Before long he'd asked her out. They got married eight weeks later.

She had achieved her dream.

'I was thinking about Roger,' she said quietly, 'about the day I met him.'

'Ah!' It was as though he saw everything.

'I thought I'd met the man of my dreams.'

'Love at first sight?'

Hardly, when it was Roger's bank balance she'd been interested in, but she wasn't admitting that. It was too embarrassing by far. She'd heard the saying that money didn't buy happiness, hadn't believed it, but now knew it was true. She'd made a foolish mistake. 'I thought so,' she answered weakly.

'So what went wrong?'

Still more questions. If she wasn't careful he'd end up hearing her life story. She'd never met a man who showed this much interest. She lifted her shoulders. 'This and that. Actually he was a control freak.' And that was putting it mildly. Roger had ruled her life.

'And I can see that you're not the type of girl who likes to be controlled,' he said with a measured smile. 'In my opinion no one should have their spirits repressed. I would never do that, especially to a woman. I like them feisty.'

And Lara Lennox was most definitely feisty. Bryce loved the way her eyes shot daggers, the proud tilt of her beautiful face, the way her tantalising body stiffened and rejected him.

He wanted to break through those defences; he wanted to show her that not all men were the same. At least her husband hadn't repressed her altogether. She'd had enough strength to get out of a marriage that wasn't working.

When Helen had invited him to this party he hadn't been sure that he'd wanted to meet her niece. Helen was an inveterate matchmaker: she'd been trying for years to find him a wife, and he was tired of her game.

If and when he ever married he wanted the girl to be of his own choosing. He wanted to make quite sure that she wasn't interested in him for all the wrong reasons. He'd had a few near misses; he'd allowed himself to be fooled by a pretty face and a willing body; he'd even almost married on one occasion, only finding out in the nick of time what she was like. He was beginning to wonder whether all women were the same: whether a rich, successful husband was their prime target in life.

This girl sitting beside him was the most intriguing he'd met in a long time. Maybe it was because she was so anti-men that he found her challenging. Maybe because she was so hauntingly beautiful. And he hadn't been lying when he'd said her skin was like the petals of an English rose.

He wanted to touch, to stroke, to feel its silken, velvety texture. The sun had never burnt it; it had never felt the incredible heat that could do so much damage here in Australia.

'Tell me,' she said now, 'have you ever been married?'

He didn't want to talk about himself; he wanted to talk about her. He wanted to find out everything. Helen had been vague, and even Lara seemed disinclined to give much away. 'No,' he answered. 'I've never found the right girl.'

'Really?' Her deep blue eyes widened. 'I find that difficult to understand.'

Did that mean she was interested in him, despite her apparent indifference? He felt a sudden hormonal surge. And then berated himself because he knew nothing about her. For all he knew she could be the same as the rest. 'It's not because I've been short of choice,' he said shortly. 'There's simply been none whom I've wished to marry.'

'You have very exacting standards, is that it?' she asked, her fine eyebrows delicately arched.

'I suppose so.'

'And you've never found Miss Perfect?'

'Not yet.' But maybe today he'd got lucky. If she took after her aunt then he'd have no complaints. Helen was a wonderful, caring woman. Money didn't mean anything to her. She always said that it was a person's mind and attitude that counted.

'This is a beautiful spot,' said Lara. 'So different to what I'm used to. I live in a town with no river or lake for miles. Water is so relaxing, don't you think?'

If you sat and looked at it, yes, he supposed. But not when you had an exciting girl by your side. 'Some people find it that way,' he agreed.

'But you don't?'

'You know what they say about familiarity.'

'I'd never get fed up of this. Nor Darling Harbour. My aunt took me there the other day. I don't know where it got its name, but it's very apt. I didn't want to come away.'

'I'm glad you like it. One of our early governors, Sir Ralph Darling, renamed it after himself. The Aborigines called it Tumbalong.' He would have liked to take her there but knew it was too soon. She was being nice for her aunt's sake, but after tonight—would she want to see him again?

For the first time in his life Bryce Kellerman felt unsure of himself.

CHAPTER TWO

FIVE days had gone by since the party and Lara had heard nothing from Bryce Kellerman. To her dismay and increasing horror she felt disappointed, and couldn't understand why since she'd made it plain that she didn't want to see him again. Wasn't she better off without a man in her life?

Helen also commented on Bryce's lack of communication. 'Perhaps he's busy. We'll give him a few more days and then invite him to dinner.'

Lara hadn't mentioned Bryce to her aunt so she knew that this was Helen up to her tricks. But even so, the thought of seeing him again sent her heart into overdrive. It also annoyed her that he'd caused a chink in her carefully erected armour. She'd need to be careful.

As it happened Helen didn't need to invite him. The next day, when they got back from a sightseeing trip, there was a message for Lara on the answering machine. 'I'd like to take you out for a meal tonight,' Bryce said, his deep, gravelly voice sending a shiver down her spine. 'I'll pick you up at eight. Any problems, give me a ring.'

Although her aunt was all of a fluster, Lara played it down. 'I don't want to go; I don't want to get involved,' she declared firmly.

Helen shook her head. 'Bryce will never hurt you.'

Maybe not! But why take risks? And yet even as she thought this Lara heard herself say, 'I suppose one date will do no harm.'

'It will give you a chance to get to know him properly,' reassured the older woman with a pleased smile. 'If I was twenty years younger I'd marry him myself.'

'Who's talking about marriage?' demanded Lara, eyes sparking indignation.

Helen grinned. 'I simply wanted to let you know what a good catch he is.'

'I came here to get over one man, not get hooked by another,' she retorted, cross with her aunt for letting her imagination work overtime.

But when Bryce came, looking devilishly handsome in grey linen trousers and a blue short-sleeved shirt, Lara couldn't stop her heart quickening. Her head told her not to get involved, to be wary every step she took, but there was no escaping the fact that he was an exciting male who aroused her in every way possible.

Not that it meant anything. Roger had thrilled her in the first few months of knowing him, and she really had thought she was in love—until she'd discovered what he was like. Her husband had stifled her feelings and emotions. He had used her. He'd made love when he'd wanted to, when he'd felt like it, her own needs and desires never entering into it. For all she knew Bryce could be the same. She daren't risk it.

For her date Lara wore a pale blue sundress with shoe-string straps and a ballerina-length skirt, her corn-gold hair tied back in a blue scrunchie, wisps of fringe softening her hairline. Her only concession to make-up was a touch of lip gloss and mascara. She didn't need anything else. Already her colour was heightened, her eyes bright with anticipation.

Bryce's smoky grey eyes made a slow, thorough inspection. 'You look stunning,' he said softly.

Lara swallowed and tried to appear nonchalant. 'This old thing, I've had it for years.'

'Whatever, the colour suits you. Hi, Helen, I promise to take good care of your niece.'

'I know you will,' said Helen with a fond smile. 'Lara has a key so you don't need to bring her back early on my account.'

Lara frowned. 'I *will* be early, Helen.'

'As you like, dear. Now you two run off and enjoy yourselves.'

Bryce's car was an old black Ford and as he opened the door for her Lara couldn't help remembering the day she had climbed into Roger Lennox's car. She'd been so pleased with herself. Nothing had warned her of what was to come. She was more wary now, more attuned to the way a man's mind worked. She had no intention of making the same mistake twice.

To her delight Bryce took her to Darling Harbour, to a seafood restaurant overlooking the water. It was magical. A myriad lights shone around them—from the buildings, from the boats, from reflections in the water, from the indigo, star-hung sky. It was perfect.

A night for romance! Lara shivered at the thought.

'Tell me about this guy who let you down so badly.' Bryce had ordered pre-dinner drinks and they'd chosen from the extensive menu.

She closed her eyes, not really wanting to talk about anything that would spoil this moment in time.

But Bryce was insistent. 'You said he was a control freak. In what way?'

Lara shrugged. 'He was a wealthy man but not a generous one. I had to account to him for breathing almost. He chose my friends, what I wore, what I did. He sold my car and kept making excuses for not buying me another, so I was trapped in the house unless he took me out. We lived miles from anywhere, not even on a bus route.'

'And you had no inkling before you married him?'

'I was swept off my feet. He owned the company I worked for. He indulged me; I was flattered; I was blinded by love.' Change that to greed, she added silently, and it would be about right. She hadn't been able to see any further than the pound signs. It was something of which she was now deeply ashamed. On the other hand it could have worked out, if Roger had been different. 'Now it's over and I don't want to talk about him. It's a part of my life I'd prefer to forget.'

'Do you still love him?'

'No!' Lara's answer was swift and fierce.

Bryce crooked a dark brow. 'It seems to me that you're not letting yourself forget him. He's there all the time, haunting your thoughts. You need a friend, someone to take you out of yourself, someone to confide in, laugh with, and enjoy the real pleasures of life.'

'And you're proposing that you should be my friend?' she said with derision. It was laughable. Bryce Kellerman didn't want to be her friend. Her lover perhaps. It was there in the way he looked at her, the way his eyes devoured her body. Were they the pleasures he was talking about? Friend? Huh! Who was he trying to kid?

'I am,' he said, his tone serious, 'if you'd let me.'

But it would be hellishly hard. How could he be a platonic friend to a woman as sexy and desirable as Lara Lennox?

It would be well-nigh impossible. He'd spent the last few days in some kind of hell. Should he see her again or shouldn't he? He'd been let down so many times that he was almost afraid to let himself care for anyone else. It was an odd feeling to be afraid when he'd made such a success of his business life. But for Lara's sake he was prepared to give it a go. She needed her faith restored in mankind.

At least that's what he kept telling himself.

She looked at him long and hard, her blue eyes probing his. 'I've never had a male friend. I didn't think it possible. I always thought that sex would rear its ugly head somewhere along the line.'

Ugly? Sex? It was the most wonderful and natural thing in the world. Obviously her husband had screwed her up on that score as well. He drew in a steadying breath, hiding the anger he felt, the questions he still wanted to ask.

'That's where you're wrong,' he said. 'Lots of women have male friends.'

'I don't know any.'

'You don't have to know them, Lara. Simply take my word for it. So what's your answer?' He held his hand out across the table. 'Friends?'

He thought she was going to refuse, had virtually resigned himself to never getting to know this stunning woman any better, decided he'd be better off for it, when slowly, and with obvious reluctance, and a great deal of courage, she slid her hand into his.

'Friends,' she agreed huskily. 'Nothing more.'

'It's a deal.' He enclosed her hand in both of his, feeling a desperate need to lean across the table and kiss her, seal their pact properly. Instead he looked deeply into her troubled eyes. What a beautiful shade of blue they were, cobalt perhaps, rich and unconsciously sultry, beckoning him without her knowledge.

His male hormones wreaked havoc. What had he done? How could he go through with this? And how could he not? This woman had captivated him from the word go.

It was with great difficulty that he released Lara's hand. He could feel her stiffening, getting ready to pull away, perhaps even regretting her decision. He smiled, a wide, friendly safe smile. 'You won't be sorry.'

'I hope not.' She fired the words at him, a warning glitter in her eyes. 'Because I have no intention of letting another man mess me around. If you hurt me, Bryce Kellerman, if you go back on your word, you'll find me a very dangerous lady. I wasn't brought up with four brothers for nothing.'

He pulled a face, pretending alarm, loving her fiery nature. 'I will never do anything to hurt you, Lara. I give you my word.' He lifted his glass. 'To us, to a true friendship.'

Lara clinked hers against it. 'To friendship.' And she allowed a slow smile to wipe the worry from her face.

She was beautiful, he thought, absolutely ravishingly beautiful. He loved everything about her: her silken hair; her delectable blue eyes; the wide, sexy mouth that absolutely begged to be kissed; her slender body that he wanted to urge against him; high, firm breasts that tempted him through the thin cotton of her dress. It would be difficult, if not impossible, to keep his hands off her.

'How long are you planning to stay?' He didn't realise how harsh his voice was until he saw her sudden frown.

'I don't know. Aunt Helen says for as long as I like.'

'Until you've got over your disastrous marriage? Is that it?'

'I guess so,' she agreed.

'Whereabouts in England do you live?' There was still so much he wanted to know.

'In the Midlands, near Birmingham. I share a flat with a friend.'

She shared! From choice or necessity? 'Did you get a settlement from your husband?' The second he'd asked he realised it was a very personal question, too personal considering they hardly knew each other. Fortunately Lara didn't seem to mind.

'I wanted nothing from him,' she announced bitterly. 'I walked into marriage with nothing, I left it with nothing. He didn't offer anything, I didn't ask. I was glad to be free of him.'

'Strong sentiments,' he agreed, 'but not very practical ones. He owed you something for the three years you gave him. Do you still work for him?'

'Goodness, no!' she exclaimed hotly. 'He made me give up my job when we got married.'

'What sort of a man is he, for God's sake?' Bryce was finding it difficult to contain his anger. 'He doesn't sound human. Didn't your feelings, your needs, your rights, enter into the equation at all?'

'Do we have to talk about this?' she asked, her eyes shooting dangerous sparks of fire.

Bryce cursed his too-ready tongue and was grateful when the waiter appeared with their entrée.

Lara's baby octopus tart served with a Kakadu plum and chilli sauce had been served at exactly the right moment.

She wished Bryce wouldn't keep questioning her. It was only friendly interest, she knew, but some things were best kept private, and her catastrophic marriage was one of them.

She ought never to have said anything, and she was definitely beginning to doubt the wisdom of agreeing to become friends. Bryce Kellerman was a dangerously sexy man; it might be impossible to hide the attraction she felt. It wasn't love, could never be love, but she couldn't rule out the possibility that she would enjoy him making love to her. In fact her body went warm at the very thought and she kept her head bent over her food so that he shouldn't see the sudden surge of colour in her cheeks.

But—so long as he stuck to his side of the bargain—there shouldn't be a problem. The trouble was, would he? Or would he fall at the first hurdle? Would they both fall? Would the temptations of the flesh be too much for them?

What had happened to the grim determination that had carried her through the dark days of her separation and divorce? She had vowed to let no other man near, not for a very long time, if ever. And now here she was, only months into her freedom, agreeing to be Bryce Kellerman's friend. What sort of a friend, for heaven's sake? A man as sexy as he couldn't possibly entertain the idea of a platonic relationship.

'You've gone very quiet.'

His deep tone startled her, made her look at him with wide, disturbed eyes. 'I'm enjoying my food.'

'You've been attacking that poor octopus as though it's still alive.'

'Oh, dear.' She smiled suddenly. 'Actually it's very delicious. How're your prawns?'

'As tasty as prawns in a lemon myrtle sauce can be,' he answered with an approving nod. 'You can never fault the food here.'

'You eat here often, then?' With other women? By himself? It was a top-class restaurant. Surely a bit out of his league?

'Only when I'm trying to impress.'

'You don't have to impress me,' she said with a quick smile. 'It's a pricey place, we can go Dutch if you like.'

He gave a disapproving wag of one finger. 'Don't insult me. I would never take out a girl if I couldn't afford it. I'm not saying I'd do it every night, but...' He let his words trail into silence.

'I'm honoured, then,' she said. 'Thank you.'

Their dishes were whipped away and their main course placed in front of them. They had decided to share a seafood platter. Lara tried to concentrate on eating but was acutely aware of Bryce watching her. Ignoring him was impossible and when their fingers touched as they both went for the same oyster, she drew back swiftly, feeling as though a savage volt of electricity had zapped through her.

His eyes asked the questions not his voice. What's the matter? What did I do?

'That was silly of me,' she said quickly. 'I'm sorry.'

'Why are you so nervous?' There was a rough edge to his tone now, a frown darkening his brow. 'Don't you think I'll keep my word?'

'Of course.' She grimaced and gave a weak smile.

'But you're not sure. You keep wondering whether

you've made a mistake.' He shook his head, mouth suddenly grim. 'Maybe you have, maybe I made the mistake. We'll call the whole thing off.'

'No!' Lara surprised herself by the quickness of her response. 'I don't want that. I could do with a friend.'

'You have your aunt.'

'Yes, but she's family, there's a difference.'

'How?'

'If I say too much to her it might get back to my mother and brothers. They don't know all the ins and outs of my marital problems. Actually my mother thought the world of Roger. She couldn't understand why I walked out on him. She did everything she could to try and persuade me to patch things up.'

'You didn't tell her the whole story?'

Lara shook her head. 'No. She'd warned me about jumping so quickly into marriage. It's what she did with my father. So I always pretended to be happy.'

'So what excuse did you give her for the divorce?'

'I just said I didn't love him any more, that the magic had gone out of the marriage and I wanted out.'

'And she believed that?' He looked faintly sceptical. 'OK, I'll accept that you can't talk to your aunt. But if you're going to behave like a skittish kitten every time we accidentally touch, then I think we have a problem, too.'

'It won't happen again,' she assured him, knowing that she sounded more confident than she felt. She wasn't even sure why she was pleading for them to remain friends. It made no sense.

As they continued to eat Bryce talked about his childhood. He was an only child and envied Lara her four brothers. 'My parents both worked and I was left to my own devices most of the time,' he said. 'I'm not saying they didn't love me, but they were so taken up with their careers that they didn't spare me much time. I was very lonely.'

'Where are they now?'

'Dad died two years ago. My mother's remarried and moved to New Zealand. He's an OK guy and she's happy enough. How about your parents?'

Lara shrugged and pulled a wistful face. 'My father walked out just after I was born. My mother brought us up on her own. She never found another man. My brothers are married now with families of their own.'

'What did she think about you coming here? Did she want to come with you?'

'She was pleased for me. Aunt Helen's my godmother and has always regretted that she's seen so little of me. But my mother's afraid of flying. She's happy with her grandchildren around her. They go and see her most days.'

'Have you any children?'

Lara shook her head emphatically. 'No, thank goodness.'

Roger had been definite about not wanting to start a family. 'I can't bear the thought of snivelling kids around me,' he'd said.

'You don't want any?' He looked at her long and hard, as if finding it difficult to understand.

'Of course I do,' she said quickly. 'I'm just glad I didn't have any with Roger. Because as sure as eggs are eggs he would have kept them from me once we divorced.'

'It might have helped your marriage.'

'Nothing could have helped that,' she said fiercely. 'It was the worst experience of my life. In fact it's doubtful I'll ever get married again.'

'That's a mistake. Not all men are like your ex.'

'Maybe not, but I'm not prepared to take the risk. I shall get a new, better paid job when I go back to England. I shall buy my own place and answer to no one.'

A faint smile lifted the corners of his mouth. 'What if you meet Mr Right? He's out there for you somewhere, you know.'

'Maybe,' she shrugged. 'I'll cross that bridge when I come to it. The way I feel at the moment men are at the bottom of my list of priorities.'

'You've allowed me into your life,' he pointed out.

Lara gave a wry smile. 'Am I crazy, or what?' Was he hinting that she couldn't be as anti-men as she proclaimed? Was he hoping that their friendship would turn into something more? Had he tricked her?

'You're not crazy, Lara.'

His warm smile made her stomach muscles bunch. This was going to be so much more difficult than she'd first thought.

'You're a very lovely lady who's gone through a hard time. And I'm going to do my best to restore your faith in mankind.'

'It'll take a lot of doing.'

'I have the time.'

Lara began to feel uncomfortable. Best change the subject. 'How did you meet my aunt? She thinks very highly of you.'

'As I do of her. She's a great character—warm, kind, witty, charitable. We met at a mutual friend's. I was fixing a door hinge and she asked whether I'd repair a broken rail on her veranda. We struck up a friendship and I go to see her whenever I can.'

'That's kind of you,' said Lara. 'Actually I think she regards you as the son she's never had. What work do you do besides helping my aunt out when she's in need?' She still couldn't believe that all he did was odd jobs. He simply didn't look the type.

'All sorts,' he declared with a vague shrug, pausing in the act of spearing a succulent prawn.

'You can't tell me you left school or college, or whatever, with no qualifications, no job in mind.' She refused to accept that.

He grinned wryly. 'Well, let's see. I started in law then decided it wasn't for me. So I took a course in electronics, then computer programming.' He studied the prawn on the end of his fork before popping it into his mouth. 'If something interests me I find out all I can about it. I suppose I'm a bit of a jack of all trades and master of none. I'm a dab hand with a drill and a saw.'

'I see. Where do you live?' The more they talked the more interested Lara became, and she was unaware that she was asking the same sort of questions that Bryce had fired at her.

'I have a little place not too far away. I'll take you there if you like?'

'Maybe one day,' she agreed. But not yet, not until she got to know him better. Her aunt might trust him but it was early days. All Lara knew was that he'd eyed her lasciviously when they'd first met, and now he'd agreed to an innocent friendship. It didn't add up.

'You still don't trust me?'

Lara was aghast that he'd read her thoughts. 'What makes you think that?'

'The look in your eyes. Your husband really did a

hatchet job on you, didn't he? It's going to be my pleasure to prove that I'm nothing like him. Tomorrow I'll pick you up and we'll go out on the harbour. Would you like that?'

Although Lara would have liked to say no, that it was too soon to spend so much time together, she found herself nodding. 'I'd love it.' He'd cleverly guessed she would be attracted by the harbour.

His smile reached out and hustled her heart into overdrive, sent a hot, warning prickle over her skin, and for the rest of the evening Lara felt an awareness that was troubling. This shouldn't be happening, she thought. I'm off men completely. What has this man got that is so compelling?

It was an easy answer. He oozed sex appeal. But it was not only that. Most men who were good-looking thought they were God's gift to women and expected to be worshipped. Bryce wasn't like that. She had thought so in the beginning but was quickly discovering her mistake.

He was forceful; he liked to get his own way—he'd shown that when he'd insisted they become friends—yet he was considerate too, more of a gentleman. He would never harm her, she was almost sure about that; her feelings would always be considered. Her aunt's recommendation had been enough, but her own gut instinct confirmed it.

At the end of the evening she felt mellow and happy, and much more relaxed than she had in a long time. Bryce dropped her off at the door with the promise to pick her up at ten the following morning. She thought he was going to kiss her, felt the rapid thud of her pulses as his head swooped low, but all he did was drop a light kiss on her brow.

'I've enjoyed this evening, Lara,' he said in his deep, toe-curling voice. 'I hope you have, too?'

She nodded, suddenly shy. 'I have, very much.'

'And I'm looking forward to tomorrow.'

'Me, too. You're very kind. You don't have to go out of your way to entertain me, you know.'

'Believe me,' he said with a slow smile, 'I wouldn't do it unless I really wanted to.'

Those magnetic, smoky eyes of his darkened as he looked at her, sent tantalising shivers down her spine, twisted her stomach into knots. It was time to go in. She turned her key in the lock. 'Goodnight, Bryce. Thank you again for a lovely evening.'

Helen was waiting up for her. Lara expected a rash of eager questions; instead her aunt said worriedly, 'I've had a phone call from your mother.'

CHAPTER THREE

LARA'S eyes shot wide. Panic set in. 'My mother is all right, isn't she? Oh, Lord, I knew I shouldn't have left her.'

'Of course she's all right,' assured her aunt quickly. 'It's just that Roger's been in touch and—'

'Roger?' queried Lara loudly. 'What the devil did he want?'

'He was asking about you. He apparently wants you back.'

'What?' Her mouth fell open; her heart slammed into her shoes. 'I wouldn't even want to be in the same room as him. I hope my mother told him where to get off. Would you mind if I rang her?'

'I said you'd do it tomorrow.'

'I'm going out with Bryce again tomorrow,' she said, remembering.

Helen beamed. 'You had a good time, then? He's lovely, isn't he?'

'Yes, he is nice,' she agreed, 'but I don't want you getting any ideas, dear aunt. We've agreed to be friends, and that's all.'

Helen's brows rose, as if to say, How can two beautiful people like you not fall in love? But she made no comment, merely smiled.

And when Lara went to bed she asked herself the same

question. How could she stop herself falling in love with Bryce Kellerman?

Lara looked in astonishment at the speedboat hitched up behind Bryce's car. 'You've surprised me. I imagined we'd be going on one of the harbour cruises.' And she couldn't help wondering how he could afford such a boat. These things didn't come cheap. Obviously doing odd jobs paid better than she'd thought.

'I wouldn't have you all to myself, then.' His voice was low and sexy and deeply meaningful.

Alarm bells rang in Lara's head. Had she underestimated this man? 'It sounds as though your motives are not entirely honourable, Bryce Kellerman,' she said sharply.

Immediately his smile faded. 'I can assure you that wasn't my intention, Lara. I thought it would be fun. But if—'

She shook her head, instantly regretting her harsh words. 'You don't have to change your plans. It's just that it wasn't what I expected.' Or was it that she was afraid of spending so much time alone with him? She had thought there would be other people around, no chance for quiet, intimate conversations such as they'd had last night.

'Good, we'll get going, then.' There was a grimness to his mouth now as though she'd annoyed him with her suspicions. And in the car he hardly spoke.

She had no idea where they were when he drew up at the water's edge, reversing expertly down the ramp. He kicked off his shoes as he let the boat slide into the water, and only then did he speak. 'Do you think you could hold the boat steady while I park the car?' he asked with exaggerated politeness.

Lara nodded, wishing she'd said nothing of her suspicions because already it was spoiling the day.

Soon they were out on the harbour, the boat bouncing over the waves as Bryce opened the throttle, and Lara loved every minute. She wished she could tell him. But his face was still set and he didn't look once in her direction.

Or so she thought. As she smoothed sun cream on her arms, legs and face, Lara was unaware that Bryce watched, that his smoky grey eyes were grave in their appraisal, that his fingers tightened on the wheel.

When Harbour Bridge came into view Bryce slowed down and they cruised gently into the harbour. It looked different from the water, the sails of the Opera House appeared first beneath the bridge, then Centre Point, the Post Office tower, the towering office blocks. It was an exciting skyline.

And then they were off again. Sometimes Bryce took his time; sometimes he skimmed the waves at breakneck speed.

The silence between them lengthened and Lara deeply regretted her earlier outburst. What should have been a pleasurable day was proving most uncomfortable. Bryce was polite but that was all. He wasn't friendly and funny and entertaining like he had been last night. And it was all her fault.

Unable to stand the tension any longer, she said quietly, 'I didn't mean to upset you.'

He looked at her then, and he slowed down, let the engine idle. 'When I said I wanted you all to myself it was a figure of speech. I had no intention of forcing you to do anything you didn't want to do. I thought it would be a pleasure.' His nostrils flared as he spoke, a tough mask over his face. 'I was forgetting that you think all men are control freaks.'

Lara winced. 'Maybe not all men.'

'But you're not prepared to give anyone else a chance.' His eyes were hard and condemning. 'If that's the case then I see no point in us continuing our—er, friendship.' He hurled the word contemptuously.

'It's not that,' she protested. Why, oh why, had she opened her mouth? 'I do want to be friends with you, Bryce. I guess I'm on edge because Roger phoned my mother yesterday.'

'Your ex?' The news brought his head up with a jerk.

Lara nodded, grimacing as she did so, letting him see how unhappy she was.

'What did he want?'

'For us to get back together.'

There was a sudden stillness about him. 'And?'

A tiny shrug lifted her slender shoulders. 'I was supposed to phone my mother back this morning. I can't believe I forgot.' She could only blame the excitement of getting ready to spend a day with Bryce! And it was true, she had been excited. She'd dithered for ages about what to wear, trying on outfit after outfit, finally settling on navy cotton shorts and a navy and white top. Helen had said she looked very nautical.

He glanced at his watch. 'She'll be in bed now. I'll remind you when we get home. Did she tell him where you are? Will he make a nuisance of himself?'

Lara hadn't even thought along those lines. Now she frowned contemplatively. 'I shouldn't think so.'

'What makes him think there's a chance that you'd go

back to him?' His voice was harsh and disapproving. 'Is there something you haven't told me?'

Lara turned her mouth down at the corners, not wanting to discuss Roger with this man. It was none of his business. But she had to say something. 'He didn't want the divorce, to tell you the truth. He couldn't understand why I felt as I did. He couldn't see anything wrong in his behaviour.'

'There's none so blind as those who don't want to see,' he said scathingly.

'You're telling me,' she declared fiercely. 'He seemed to think that because he bought me nice things, because we had a comfortable home, because we entertained his friends on a fairly regular basis, that I had a good and fulfilling life. He didn't realise that I'd have liked my own friends around me, that I'd have liked a say in some things. He had no idea how stifled I felt.'

'It's a shame he's spoilt your holiday,' said Bryce. 'Last night you began to relax. Today you're as uptight as when I first met you. You've rebuilt the wall. I'm an outsider.'

Lara gave a rueful smile. 'I didn't mean for that to happen. I appreciate the trouble you've gone to on my behalf. I'm enjoying today.'

A dark eyebrow quirked upwards. 'Are you sure?'

'Absolutely.' She had only herself to blame for the tension that had settled over them like a thundercloud.

'Are you ready for lunch?'

Lara looked around at all the water surrounding them. 'Where are you suggesting we eat?'

'You have two choices,' he said, his smile warmer now. 'We could go to Doyles at Watsons Bay—you've heard of our famous fish-and-chip restaurant? Or we could drop anchor and eat right here. I have a hamper in the cabin.'

'I think I'd like the picnic,' Lara decided. She no longer wanted to be surrounded by other people. She was enjoying Bryce's company too much.

'You're not afraid of me any more?' he asked, eyes narrowed.

'It was silly of me to be wary,' she said with a wry, apologetic smile. 'I should have known differently.'

And so out came the cool-box filled with thick slices of ham and chunky chicken portions, with salads and cheeses, with bread rolls and wine, and for dessert a mango already sliced, glossy plums and finger bananas, as well as several different flavoured yoghurts. Far too much for them, but all utterly, utterly delicious.

'This is wonderful,' she said more than once. 'You're certainly doing me proud today.'

'I would always do you proud if you were mine,' he said seriously. 'I would never treat you like a possession.' Although his eyes were grave they managed to send sensual messages at the same time. Her skin grew warm; her fingers clenched around the wineglass, and so that she didn't need to look at him she swallowed what was left in one gulp.

Immediately he refilled her glass, his own too, and they sat in companionable silence for a few minutes. Other craft moved past them, their occupants either waving or calling out a greeting—he seemed to know many people—but they didn't intrude on their privacy.

'You're not thinking of going back to Roger?' he asked at length.

'Goodness, no!' she exclaimed. 'It's the last thing I want.'

'Sometimes men like your ex wield a power that a woman finds hard to resist.'

Lara shook her head. 'Getting away from that marriage was the best thing I ever did.'

Eventually Bryce said it was time they moved and he pulled up the anchor, but when he turned the key nothing happened. The engine groaned but refused to start. He swore beneath his breath.

Was a boat engine like a car engine? Lara wondered, and then cursed. Dammit, she hadn't wanted to think about Roger again. Why did he keep intruding into her thoughts? It was the phone call, of course, one she could have easily done without. And until she rang her mother she wouldn't know exactly what he had said—and he would continue to plague her.

She watched as Bryce lifted the engine cover and fiddled with leads and wires before he tried it again. Still no joy. But at least he looked as though he knew what he was doing. When the engine finally sprang into life he gave a grunt of satisfaction.

'What was wrong?' she asked.

'I suspect the fuel pump. It's not the first time it's done this on me. In fact...' He let his voice trail away.

'In fact what?' she asked with a frown.

'I think I should pull into shore and check it out. Better to be safe than sorry.'

All Lara could see on the shoreline were private houses, large exclusive mansions worth millions of dollars with steeply terraced gardens leading down to the water's edge. She'd been studying them as they'd eaten their lunch, wondering what sort of people lived there.

'I can't see anywhere you can tie up.'

'That's simple. I live there.' He pointed to one of the elegant properties.

Lara frowned. 'What do you mean, you live there?' Dread filled her. He would need to be fantastically rich to live in one of those houses. And if this was the case why hadn't he told her? Why hadn't Helen told her? Bryce had convinced her that he was a man she could trust; she had begun to relax with him, feel happy in his company—and now this!

Bryce saw her changing expressions and laughed. 'I live in a converted loft above that boathouse.'

Lara followed his pointing finger. And there, poking out from behind a fancy cruiser, she saw it. 'You mean you—rent the loft?'

'Actually it comes free with the job,' he admitted, sounding a trifle self-conscious.

'It must be some job,' she said, her eyes widening with surprise at the same time as relief washed over her. 'What are you, a permanent handyman there?'

'In a manner of speaking, but I also tinker about with boats. They're my driving passion. This guy owns a fleet. He keeps me pretty busy.'

'For the moment, you mean,' she said with a laugh, realising how wrong she had been to mistrust him. 'Until something else takes your fancy.'

'How well you're getting to know me,' he answered, with a laugh of his own.

'Your boss must be fabulously wealthy to live in a place like that.' It was easily the largest house in the area. She wondered what he was like, this man Bryce did so much work for. Had wealth gone to his head, made him feel he was better than anyone else?

Bryce's boat looked like a poor second cousin as he tied up beside the handsome cruiser. Perhaps it wasn't even his. Perhaps it too belonged to the owner of the house. And he certainly couldn't be too much of an ogre if he let Bryce live here rent-free.

He helped her out and as their hands locked Lara felt a surge of desire flood through her. She tried to ignore it, didn't even snatch away, although she was tempted. Instead she kept her eyes down and prayed Bryce hadn't noticed her reaction. She suspected that he wouldn't need much encouragement.

When he let her go she drew in a painful breath of relief, annoyed with herself for letting such feelings surface. And yet, how could she have stopped them when she hadn't known they existed? Nothing had happened today to stimulate such desire. Bryce had been the perfect gentleman. So where had these feelings come from?

She was given no time to dwell on it. Bryce led the way up some steep wooden steps to the converted loft space. The main house itself was on the hillside above them and couldn't be seen.

'What a lovely spot,' she declared enthusiastically. 'You're so lucky.' And she deliberately pushed all other thoughts out of her head.

'It suits my purpose,' he agreed.

'It would suit me, too,' she informed him. 'I'd never look for anywhere else to live.' The walls and ceiling were timber lined; the floor was wooden too with scattered rugs. A counter unit divided the huge living area from the kitchen, and an open staircase led to an apexed, galleried bedroom with a bathroom leading off. Only the bathroom had any privacy. But for one man on his own it was perfect.

It was definitely a man's place: simple, clean, uncluttered lines; solid, practical furniture. Everything had its use; nothing was allowed in that didn't serve a purpose.

'Help yourself to a drink while I see to the boat. I shouldn't be long.'

'Maybe I could help?' she suggested hopefully.

'And get those beautiful hands dirty. I don't think so. This is men's work.'

Lara stuck her hands on her hips and looked at him fiercely. 'Is that chauvinism? You're forgetting my brothers. I was one of them or I was out. I can do anything a man can do.'

'Really?' Her outburst sent his lips curving in amusement. 'I'll remember that one of these days. For the moment, though, sit down and look beautiful. I shouldn't be long.'

But Lara couldn't relax; she stepped out onto the veranda that ran the width of the loft and looked down at Bryce. Her breath caught in her throat. He'd stripped off his shirt and as he leaned over the engine powerful muscles flexed beneath darkly tanned skin. His shoulders were wide, his hips narrow, and she saw a power and strength that she'd only guessed at. It did strange things to her, knotting muscles and quickening pulses, and it became increasingly clear that Bryce Kellerman was beginning to creep beneath her skin. She turned back into the room, needing to escape while she could still breathe.

It was a perfect place to live. Why would anyone want

to buy a huge house full of rooms that were rarely used? This was spacious enough to entertain and yet small enough to look after with the minimum of fuss.

Even in the kitchen there was everything to make life easy, a huge fridge and freezer standing side by side, a dishwasher, washing machine, microwave, a double oven with separate hob. It was a dream kitchen. I could work in here, she thought, and never want for anything.

So engrossed was Lara that she didn't hear Bryce come up the stairs and enter the apartment, wasn't even aware of his presence until she turned around—and cannoned into him.

Instinctively she put her hands out to steady herself and felt firsthand those powerful muscles, felt the hardness and warmth of his body. And again desire flared through her—hot, instant desire. It ripped through her body like an exploding firework.

Involuntarily she looked up into Bryce's face—and saw her own raw need mirrored there. Move, before it's too late, she ordered, before something happens that you'll regret, but she was incapable even of speaking, much less retreating.

It felt like for ever that she stood there touching him, her palms burning, her heartbeats racing, her eyes locked into his. And even when she heard him groan, saw his head bow down towards her, she could do nothing about it except wait for the inevitable.

When, with another groan, one sounding like despair this time, he backed away from her, shot away in fact, it came as a distinct shock. 'Why did you have to do that?' he asked harshly.

Lara felt bemused all of a sudden and shook her head.
'Do what?'

'Touch me like that, dammit.'

Bryce's belly was on fire, his pulses jerked uncontrollably,
and it had taken every ounce of his not inconsiderable will-
power to back out of the situation that had begun to look
so promising.

He knew that Lara would have hated him for it afterwards. She might not have been able to help herself in that
instant—it was one of those moments of madness that
crept up on most people at some time or another—but
she'd made her feelings crystal clear.

If he dared go beyond the bounds of friendship he would
lose her altogether. Much as he might want to make love
to her, hold her in his arms and feel that wonderfully sexy
body against his, he had to be patient. Even if it meant a
long, ice-cold shower every time he left her.

'I wasn't touching you.' She spat the words back. 'Not in
the way you mean. I was simply steadying myself. You're a
fool to yourself if you took it to mean anything else.'

She looked beautiful, blue eyes flashing, cheeks an angry red, her whole body pulsating. She would never have
admitted it, he knew, but that moment of contact had disturbed her as much as it had him. If he'd given in to temp-
tation she would have returned his kiss with the passion
she was strongly trying to deny.

He tried to control his deepened breathing, tried to take
his eyes away from her, but it was like attempting to stem
a tidal flow. 'You took long enough about moving.' He
grunted. 'It looked to me like an invitation.' It wasn't true,
but it was his best form of defence. 'If that's the type of

relationship you want, why don't you be honest with yourself and admit it?'

Lara shook her head angrily and turned her back on him, hands splayed on the counter top, not even deigning to answer. She was rigid from head to foot—and it was entirely his fault! He cursed himself for his stupidity. He should have backed away the instant she fell against him; he should never have allowed time for desire to erupt—except that it had been so instant he could have done nothing about it.

'Is the boat ready?' she asked raggedly.

She'd had enough of his company! She wanted to go home! She probably never wanted to see him again! He pulled a wry face, fists clenched at his side. 'Almost. I came up for a drink. Would you like one?' Trying to appear normal, almost impossible considering the state of his hormones, Bryce opened the fridge and took out an ice-cold can.

'No, thanks.' It was a tight, tiny voice, still shutting him out, still telling him in no uncertain terms that she disapproved of his behaviour.

'Well, there's one here if you want it.' He left the room; he couldn't remain there watching her hating him. The whole day had started wrongly and he blamed it on Roger. If the damn man hadn't upset her none of this would have happened.

Why on earth would he go through with a divorce and then want her back? It didn't make sense. And how much of the truth was he ever likely to learn? Lara could have been exaggerating. He might be a very nice guy. It might be that she hadn't been ready for marriage and had felt the

constraints, had regretted losing her carefree, single status.
It did happen.

He gulped down the drink and threw the can in the bin,
then tried to concentrate on what he was doing. He hadn't
really needed to go upstairs to get a drink when there was
one in the cool-box. But he had sensed Lara looking down
at him and it had created urges. Urges he could do nothing
about, but at least he could be near her.

It was a ridiculous state of affairs. He was treading on
dangerous ground. He wasn't even being perfectly honest
with her. Yet she was getting beneath his skin like no other
woman ever had, and time spent apart was like being under
the surgeon's knife with no anaesthetic.

He worked feverishly, trying to shut her out of his mind,
but it was impossible. The merest thought sent his testosterone levels rising. The best thing he could do would be
to take her back to Helen's and then forget her. There was
no hope for him. This friendship thing wasn't working.
She was too dangerously attractive.

He'd tried—he hadn't given it very long, admittedly—
but this latest incident had proved how unattainable such
a friendship was. Why he'd suggested it in the first place
he didn't know. He'd wanted her from the second he'd
clapped eyes on her. How could he have even contem-
plated settling for anything less?

As soon as the new fuel pump was connected and all
was running sweetly he washed his hands beneath the outside tap before running up to the loft apartment, this time
taking care to let her know he was coming.

Lara was reading a magazine. A man's magazine! Or
maybe she was pretending to read it. She looked up as he
entered, her expression cool and disinterested. 'Ready?'

'I need a shower,' he said, disappointment that she was still annoyed with him making his tone curt. It didn't bode well for the homeward journey.

The icy shower didn't help much either. It didn't reach the heart of him where need and desire continued to rage. It didn't quell any of his sexual urges. And when he came out of the bathroom, a thick navy towel wrapped around his loins, he couldn't resist looking over the balustrade.

Lara was pacing the room but she must have heard him because she looked up, and a look of horror crossed her face. She turned away quickly, but not quickly enough. She might try to deny her feelings, but her expression gave her away every time.

It was a shame that she was so afraid to let down her defences. One bad experience shouldn't be allowed to put her off men for the rest of her life, he thought, as he vigorously towelled himself dry. But what could he do about it?

The answer was nothing. The solution lay within her. Perhaps it was too soon. Perhaps he should give her time to settle down. A new country, a new man, it must be unnerving.

He hopped from foot to foot as he pulled on a clean pair of shorts. The trouble was, if he gave her the space she seemed to need, he might lose her. Not that he'd got her yet, but he felt there was hope—if he remained patient. But to do nothing, and allow that wretch to waltz back into her life would be unthinkable.

He was in a no-win situation. He needed to work fast but Lara wouldn't allow it. His thoughts were deeply troubled as he joined her. 'Let's go,' he said abruptly.

Lara was angry with herself for ruining what had promised to be a perfect friendship. Why couldn't she have laughed when she'd bumped into Bryce? Why couldn't she have said, Oops, sorry! and moved away? It would have been the natural thing to do. It's what people did in such circumstances.

Instead she'd made a fool of herself. And now Bryce was cross with her and it didn't bode well for the trip home. All in all it hadn't been a very successful day.

He didn't bounce the boat across the waves as he had on the outward journey. It was a sedate ride, a steady ride. His brow was furrowed and he was deep in thought. The boat seemed to be almost driving itself.

She ought to apologise, she supposed—again—but it had been partly his fault, too. He could have moved away. He needn't have stood there looking as though he was ready to devour her.

'How long are you going to sulk?' she asked crossly, the words out before she'd even considered them.

He turned swiftly to look at her. 'Forgive me, Lara, but if anyone's at fault here, it's you.'

'Trust a man to pass the buck,' she retorted. 'Always thinking they can never do anything wrong.'

'Is that so?' Grey eyes were no longer smoky and soft but as hard as chips of granite. 'Let's analyse this thing. You bumped into me. You didn't move. And yet I get the blame. Where is the logic in that?'

'You're splitting hairs.' She tossed back the words, more furious with herself for opening this conversation than with Bryce.

'I think we should forget the whole thing.'

'How can I when you were on the verge of kissing me?' she demanded heatedly.

'You're saying you didn't want me to? It's not how it looked to me, Lara. I think you wanted it very much indeed.'

'I did not,' she answered indignantly. 'I was waiting for you to back away. It would have been the gentlemanly thing to do.'

'I think we're making mountains out of molehills here.' And still his eyes hadn't softened, still they stabbed into her with all the ferociousness of a cornered lion.

Suddenly the deep, insistent tone of a ship's horn penetrated their minds. Lara realised that it had been going for sometime but neither of them had taken any notice, far too intent on their own fierce argument to let extraneous sounds intrude. Now, she saw to her horror that they were heading straight for one of the ferries that regularly ploughed these waters.

Bryce hissed out an oath and swung the boat over. They missed it by a hair's breadth. Lara clapped her hands to her mouth, her whole body shaking. 'That was my fault.'

'No.' Bryce looked shaken, too. 'I should have looked where I was going.'

'God, I thought we were going to hit it.'

'It was a close shave.' He drew in a deep, steadying breath. 'Are you all right?'

'I will be in a minute.'

'Come here.'

With no thought of refusing she slid over on to the seat beside him and he draped an arm around her shoulders while he kept his other hand on the wheel. There wasn't really room for two and she was squashed against him, thigh touching thigh, skin touching skin. But amazingly she didn't feel threatened.

'I'm so sorry to put you through that,' he declared softly. 'I'm not usually so inattentive.'

'You can't take all the blame,' she said, shaking her head. 'I started the argument instead of letting things lie. I'm sorry, too.'

'Apology accepted,' he muttered. 'How about we forget it and start over again?'

'I'd like that,' she said. She didn't want to lose his friendship. She was—and this surprised her deeply—beginning to depend on him. She was content in his company—most of the time. It was only when sexual attraction reared its head that she started to get worried. And so long as they avoided such situations—if that were possible—then there was no reason why they couldn't become really good friends.

When her body stopped trembling he let her go and she moved back to the relative safety of her own seat, even though she'd have liked to stay by him a while longer. It would have been dangerous, of course. As they both relaxed, other, more insidious, feelings would have crept in and spoilt their camaraderie.

'It's been quite a day.'

She wasn't sure whether Bryce was speaking to her or himself so she remained silent, and by the time they got back to where they'd parked the car Lara was feeling more content.

It was wrong to allow anything to spoil her pleasure of being on Sydney Harbour. It had to be the most beautiful harbour in the world. It was Australia's proud claim and she was inclined to agree.

'I hope that, on the whole, you've enjoyed your day,' he said as they drew up outside Helen's house.

'I have. I love being on the water.'

'Then we must do it again.'

Lara nodded. 'I'd like that.' And she really meant it. The almost kiss had faded now, perhaps to be resurrected later when she was on her own, but for the moment she was content in Bryce's company.

'Thank you for making today special, Lara.' As he spoke Bryce leaned towards her, his eyes darkening with intent.

CHAPTER FOUR

LARA was thankful that Helen was out. Her heated cheeks and the panic in her eyes would have told her aunt everything. She really had thought that Bryce was going to kiss her and although she had wanted his kiss she knew it would have proved fatal. It would have told him how she felt and there would have been no going back.

Without a word she had leapt out of the car and had raced into the house, and now she leaned back against the door breathing deeply, trying to steady her shattered nerves. Despite all her good intentions, Bryce Kellerman was getting beneath her skin. She wasn't sure she could handle it.

Not until Lara heard his car pull away was she finally able to move. She poured herself a generous vodka and tonic. In a minute she would ring her mother, but for the moment all she could think about was Bryce Kellerman.

Had he been going to kiss her, properly kiss her, she wondered, as she gulped her drink, or was it all in her mind? Had she panicked for nothing? He was definitely a sensually exciting man. It would be difficult if not impossible to remain friends and ignore his sexuality. So why was she going out with him? Why was she lining up a whole heap of trouble for herself?

She had no answer.

Time for her phone call.

'Hi, Mum, it's me.'

'Lara!' exclaimed Vera excitedly. 'At last. I thought you were never going to ring me.'

'I've been busy, Mum. How are you?' The line was as clear as if her mother was in the next room.

It was a few minutes before Lara was able to ask the question that was troubling her. 'I hear you had a phone call from Roger?'

A slight pause, a telling pause. 'Yes.'

'What did he say exactly?' she asked, although she knew what her mother was going to say. You should never have broken up; he's still in love with you, Lara. Give him another chance.

'He's in a whole heap of trouble, Lara.'

'Oh?' She couldn't hide her surprise.

'He's been accused of rape. You and I both know he isn't capable of that, but it's what the girl's claiming. She's taking him to court.'

Oh, but he *was* capable. Lara knew that from personal experience. Maybe technically he hadn't raped her because they'd been married, but he'd used her body when she had been unwilling. She'd been too young and naïve, too anxious to preserve her marriage, to do anything about it. 'You're my wife and I can do as I like,' he would say. But her mother knew nothing of this. It wasn't something Lara was proud of. She'd stuck it for as long as she could but there had come a time when she'd had to get out.

'He wants you to give him a character reference. He says you're the only one who can help him.'

Like hell she would. If he'd committed the crime then he deserved to be punished. In fact it would give her much pleasure to hear that he'd been found guilty. It was what he deserved.

'I've given him Helen's phone number.'

'You've done *what*?' Lara shrieked. 'You had no right. I don't want him ringing me here. If he's got himself into trouble then it's up to him to get himself out of it. I can't help.'

'Really, Lara,' said Vera sharply. 'It's the very least you can do.'

'You don't know the half, Mother. I got out of that marriage because—well, because Roger wasn't the man I thought he was. I can't help him. Please tell him not to ring me here.'

'What is it you're not telling me?'

Lara heard the concern in her parent's voice. 'I don't want to talk about it,' she said firmly, shaking her head. 'Let's just say he didn't treat me all that well and I'm glad to be rid of him.' And no matter how much her mother asked Lara refused to be drawn any further.

When Helen came home Lara was in bed. It was barely ten o'clock, but she hadn't wanted her aunt's inevitable questions. She'd pushed all thoughts of Roger out of her mind and had allowed entrance the more pleasurable feelings of her day out with Bryce.

Initially she'd wanted to forget him as well, but it was impossible. He crept into her thoughts whether she wanted him to or not. Although she knew that she dared not let him take over her life, she could not help but be excited by him. He intoxicated her—being with him was like drinking a heady wine—and sooner or later she knew that their platonic friendship would burst into something more. Neither of them would be able to stop it.

Hopefully that wouldn't happen too soon. She needed time to accustom herself to the idea, prepare for it, decide how to handle it. At the moment she wasn't ready for a full-on relationship; a little flirting, yes, the odd kiss or two, perhaps, but nothing heavy, nothing involved, nothing deep and meaningful.

Over breakfast the following morning Helen asked so many questions about her day with Bryce that Lara began to lose patience.

'And when is he taking you out again?' her aunt probed.

'I've no idea,' Lara said shortly. 'We made no plans.'

'I bet it won't be long before he's on the phone,' said Helen knowingly. As if on cue, it rang. Helen's smile widened. 'There, what did I tell you?'

Lara's heart quickened its beat. She might pretend indifference, but deep down it was another matter altogether.

But it wasn't Bryce after all.

'That was an old school friend of mine,' explained Helen. 'Her daughter's planning to backpack around Australia and she wants to know if I can put her up for a few days. Of course I said yes. You don't mind, do you? I love filling my house with young people. I deeply regret that Tom and I never had children.'

'Why didn't you?' asked Lara. It was something she'd often wondered.

Helen gave a wry shrug. 'Tom was infertile. We did talk about adoption, but it wasn't something either of us really wanted. We thought we'd have each other for ever and that would be enough.'

'I'm sorry.'

'Don't be, I'm happy now, in my own way. But don't make my mistake, Lara. Fill your house with children.'

'When I find the right man,' said Lara with a faint smile.

'I think you might have already done that.'

Lara refused to answer, refused even to look at her aunt. It was far too soon to be thinking along such lines.

Although when Bryce rang later she couldn't stop the sudden rush of emotions that convoluted her stomach and sent her mind into a frenzy. Bryce was far too electrifying a man to be a mere friend. She ought to have known that from the beginning. Their relationship was going to be all or nothing. He would never settle for anything less, no matter what he said or how hard he tried, and she couldn't see herself doing it either.

'Are you listening to me, Lara?' he asked.

'Yes. No! What did you say?'

'Have I called at a bad time?'

No time is a good time where you're concerned, she said silently. 'Of course not.'

'So how about it?'

Lara hadn't the faintest idea what Bryce was talking about. When she'd answered the phone all she could think about was the way her body was reacting to the gravelly tones of his voice, the tingling heat that invaded her. How could she listen to what he was saying when she felt as if she was on fire?

'I've just invited you to dinner tonight.'

'You don't have to do that,' she said quickly, perhaps too quickly. 'I'm sure there are other things you'd rather be doing.'

'I was inviting both you and Helen.'

'Oh!' He'd guessed how she'd felt when she'd fled from him yesterday. Had known that he'd stirred her senses in a way she hadn't expected and hadn't wanted? Did he think she'd feel safe with her aunt there? Or was it that *he* needed a third person present? He needed protecting from his own headstrong feelings? 'I didn't realise you meant that,' she said. 'Let me just ask Helen.'

Her aunt's answer was a foregone conclusion.

Bryce sounded pleased. 'Bring your swimmers. I have permission to use the pool whenever I like.'

The house was hidden from the road by a high wall and iron gates and Lara could see no way down to the boathouse except through them. But even as they pulled up the gates opened and Bryce appeared.

Her heart did its customary flip. All he wore was a pair of brief white shorts, and the sight of those long tanned legs and deeply muscled chest with its whorls of dark hair was almost her undoing. Everything went into overdrive and she was far too aware of him for her own good.

He briefly acknowledged Helen before his eyes locked into Lara's. 'Welcome; it's good to see you again,' he said, as though it had been days instead of twenty-four hours.

She turned to her aunt, needing to drag her eyes away before they fell out of their sockets. Thank goodness she was not going to be alone with him. But Helen had her hand clapped over her mouth. 'What's the matter?' Lara asked anxiously.

'I've just remembered that I'm supposed to be somewhere else. Oh, dear.'

'It's a bit late now,' Lara pointed out. 'Why don't you ring and explain that—?'

'I can't,' her aunt cut in quickly. 'It's very important and better late than never. I can't imagine how I forgot. Bryce, darling, you will excuse me, won't you?'

Lara looked suspiciously from Helen to Bryce, wondering if this was a set-up. But Bryce too looked surprised. Though it changed quickly to pleasure. 'You hurry along, Helen. I'll see to it that Lara gets home safely.'

And when Helen had gone he said, 'This is going to be a better evening than I expected.'

Lara lifted a brow. 'Did you know that Helen was going to back out at the last minute?'

'Of course I didn't know,' he declared strongly. 'But I'm not saying I'm sorry.' And his smoky eyes darkened as they brazenly roved over her, right from the tips of her bronze-painted toenails, over the lemon cotton button-through dress, lingering a moment on the curves of her breasts, causing her nipples to peak, giving away her inner tension, then moving right up to the dark blonde hair framing her face. And finally his eyes reached hers.

'I'll stay on one condition,' she said, doing her hardest not to look away, though Lord knew it was hard. He sent the wickedest thoughts through her mind.

'That I keep my hands off you.' He guessed, with a heavy sigh. 'It's OK, I know the rules. Let's go down and get a drink.'

They passed the impressive, sprawling mansion with its landscaped, terraced gardens. There wasn't a soul in sight. Why someone would buy a place like this and not use it to its full potential Lara couldn't begin to understand. She saw a tennis court and putting green, and the Olympic-sized pool which, she had to admit, looked very tempting.

It was here that Bryce stopped. Huge cream canvas sails shaded the terrace. A table was set up with three chairs around it and three deep blue glasses on it, proving, at least, that he'd been expecting Helen to stay.

* * *

'I have wine keeping cool,' Bryce informed her. 'Would you like some now, or after your swim?' He couldn't believe his good fortune in getting Lara to himself. He couldn't have orchestrated it any better if he'd tried.

It had crossed his mind that Helen might have done it deliberately. If so, good for her. If not, it had still worked to his advantage.

When Lara had turned away from him yesterday and fled into the house as though he'd been about to savage her, he'd been stunned. She couldn't have made her feelings any clearer. And yet it still hadn't stopped him inviting her out again—and she had accepted. So perhaps things weren't as black as they looked.

'I think after,' Lara said.

'So we'll swim. There are changing rooms over there.' He indicated a low white building. And he would be able to see at long last her slender curves that were driving him crazy. They would play in the water; perhaps their bodies would even touch. He wanted her so much. Not as a friend, but as a lover. He desired her as he had no other woman.

'I already have my swimsuit on,' she told him and self-consciously began unbuttoning her dress.

It wasn't often a woman was shy in front of him—usually they enjoyed flaunting their bodies—and he found it a refreshing change. What he would have liked to do was unbutton the dress for her. The mere thought of it sent a surge through his loins. He would do it very slowly, savouring each ravishing inch as it was exposed to his greedy eyes. Of course it would be much better if she was naked underneath. He could touch and stroke and kiss, acquaint himself with every irresistible part of her.

He hadn't realised that he was staring, that his lust was

naked in his eyes, until Lara gave a cry of distress and turned her back on him. Dammit! He wasn't doing a very good job of gaining her confidence.

Cursing his stupidity he swung away and dived cleanly into the water, his strokes long and strong as they took him away from the temptress who was turning his life upside down. Then he drew in a deep breath and did a whole length under water. When he looked for Lara she was nowhere in sight, and for just a minute he thought he had scared her away.

Suddenly she surfaced a few feet from him and shook her hair out of her eyes. She looked gorgeous with it plastered to her head and her skin glowing, and as she looked at him she laughed. 'Let's have a race.'

Relieved that she'd forgotten her earlier distress he nodded. 'Do you want a head start?'

'Definitely not.' There was a challenge in her lovely blue eyes. 'If I win I want it to be fair and square.'

He didn't see how she could win. But he'd forgotten how tall Lara was, how long her arms, and she powered through the water with as much strength as most men. He was amazed—and impressed. She didn't actually win but he didn't beat her by very much.

'You're good,' he said admiringly, as they both struggled for breath.

'I swam for my school.'

'You should have taken it up as a career. You could have swum for your country.'

Lara shook her head. 'I enjoy it, yes, but it was never my burning ambition.'

'So what was?' She seemed relaxed for once, enjoying the water, enjoying his company. Being together.

But all of a sudden that changed. She turned her head away and mumbled, 'I didn't have one.' And she struck off again across the pool.

Now what had he said to upset her? Perhaps someone, or something, had thwarted her ambition, whatever that had been. Perhaps he'd touched on a sore point. But if he had, why couldn't she talk about it?

Bryce let her swim alone, watching her, admiring her fluid strokes, wishing she'd open up to him, let him into her life. He hated having this wall between them. Every time he thought he'd almost climbed to the top, she knocked him down again. Not that he was faint-hearted—he intended winning Lara if it was the last thing he did—but it looked as though it was going to be a long, hard struggle.

After a few minutes he joined her, gliding alongside, his body almost touching hers, but not quite, and she didn't move away. They played like porpoises, skimming the water, skimming each other, rolling, diving, though never once did he let their bodies meet. He found it erotic and exciting though he wasn't quite sure whether Lara felt the same. She was laughing, admittedly, and her eyes were bright, and she looked so beautifully sexy that he wanted to make love to her right there in the water.

When she struck out for the side he felt intense disappointment.

'I'm exhausted.' She lifted heavy arms to show what she meant. 'I must be out of condition.'

Or running scared. She clearly wasn't as immune to him as she tried to make out. Swimming around each other had been a kind of foreplay. And the longer they played the more aroused she'd become.

If he taxed her she'd deny it, but she'd given herself away. She'd been more breathless than the exercise called for. He'd seen her breasts heaving; he'd seen hunger and need glittering in those magnificent cobalt eyes. And now she had a desperate wish to hide it from him.

'Is there somewhere I can shower?' she asked as he hauled himself out to join her, and he noticed that she tried not to meet his eyes.

He hid his disappointment, smiling instead. 'Come, I'll show you.'

She had a stunningly beautiful body. Well-toned, slender but not too slim, rounded in all the right places. Her swimsuit was an azure blue, almost matching her eyes, cut high at the legs, making them look longer than they already were, and dipping low at the front to reveal tantalising curves that he had trouble looking away from.

His thoughts were positively indecent and he didn't know for how much longer he could keep his hands off her.

Lara was impressed with the shower and changing rooms. There were four in all, beautifully tiled in aquamarine and, as she showered in the end one, she could hear Bryce using one of the others.

She couldn't help visualising his naked body. Amazingly she wanted to touch him; she wanted to slip into the cubicle with him and slide her hands over his sexy, hard-boned body. She wanted to feel, to touch, to experience. And she wanted him to touch her! The very thought made her mouth run dry.

She held her head back and, closing her eyes, let the water stream onto her face and down over her taut breasts.

Breasts that ached for his touch. And this was only the beginning of the evening! She finished her shower quickly, grabbed the towel, and wrapped it tightly around her, as if by so doing she could quell the unwanted urges that tormented her body.

By the time Bryce had finished his shower she was fully dressed, standing at the side of the pool, waiting. It had grown dark and lights had come on both in the pool and in the grounds around it, glowing softly, giving the whole place a magical air. It was so beautiful she could have stayed there for ever.

Although his feet were silent Lara sensed Bryce approach, knew exactly when he stood behind her. She even tensed herself for his touch, but it didn't happen.

'Let's go and see how dinner's doing,' he said. 'Are you hungry?' There was nothing in his voice to suggest that he'd been having similarly indecent thoughts, although in the water, when he'd swum at her side, she'd been almost sure that he was as turned on as she was. If so he was hiding it well and she supposed she ought to be grateful. She wished that she had the same iron control.

Turning to follow him Lara's throat tightened. All that preserved Bryce's modesty was a towel draped low on his hips. It was almost a certainty that he had nothing on underneath. She ran the tip of her tongue over suddenly dry lips and tried to look away. For some reason her head refused to budge.

'Are you allowed to use the pool any time?' Her voice came out in a squeak and she prayed he wouldn't ask her what was wrong.

'Whenever I like,' he agreed.

How lucky could he get?

As she followed Bryce down the steep flight of steps to the boathouse, Lara couldn't take her eyes off him. The lamps that lit their path accentuated his hard muscles, outlined the fantastic shape of him, and made him seem—if it were possible—more desirable than ever. She swallowed the sudden lump that came to her throat, thought again about what was beneath that carefully arranged towel, and asked herself why she was denying her body what it so obviously wanted.

'I wish Helen had a pool.' She wondered whether Bryce could feel her eyes burning into his back, whether he was aware of the torment he was putting her through.

'You can always use this one,' he offered casually.

And join him in the water again! She liked the sound of it. But what she said was, 'It's too far away. In any case I wouldn't dare use it if you weren't here. Can you imagine the owner coming home and finding a strange woman in his pool?'

Bryce glanced over his shoulder and grinned. 'I'm sure he'd be delighted. In any case, he's very generous and understanding.'

It was the look in those smouldering eyes that did it. They'd met hers for only a second but it was enough to send her weak and shaky, and whether she tripped, or whether her legs gave way, she wasn't sure, but she suddenly and alarmingly felt herself falling forwards.

Her panicky cry alerted Bryce and in an instant he had swung around. His arms came out to stop her, but she fell so heavily that she took him with her. They crashed down a couple of steps and then hit the side retaining wall and came to an abrupt halt.

'Are you all right?' he asked, his arms still protectively around her, neither of them trying to move.

'I think so.'

'What happened?'

'I don't know.'

'I've had plenty of women fall for me but none as heavily as you.' A complacent grin accompanied his words.

Lara huffed and tried to get up, ignoring the pain that shot through her arm. There was more truth in his words than he knew.

'Whoa there. Take it easy,' he said. 'Let me help you. Even if nothing's broken, you're sure to be shook up.'

And so together they got to their feet, Bryce's ready hands lifting and steadying, his naked body brushing excitingly against her. Amazingly the towel had stayed in place! Desire pulsated through her and goodness knew what Bryce must have thought when he felt her body heat.

But when she tried to push herself away the pain in her arm was so intense that she cried out.

'What's wrong?' Bryce's concern was instant.

'I think I fell on my arm. It hurts like the devil.'

'Here, let me look. No, better still, we'll go indoors. Can you walk? Nothing else hurting?'

'No.' She nursed her bad arm with her good one, but even so Bryce slid his arm around her waist to make sure that she didn't fall again. Lara liked being held by this man, liked the feel of his hard, nude, masculine body, and the clean, fresh smell that was essentially Bryce. It was worth being injured just for this moment.

He pushed open the door to his loft house and a delicious smell of cooking made their nostrils quiver, reminding Lara how hungry she was. Bryce sat her down on the couch. 'Now, let's take a look.'

He knelt in front of her and his fingers were gentle as they experimentally and expertly felt her arm.

'Do you know what you're doing?' she asked, not really caring. He could touch her all over if he liked the way she was feeling at this moment.

'I know,' he confirmed. 'And I'm not happy. I think you've broken it. You need an X-ray.'

'Don't be silly!' exclaimed Lara, all tender thoughts flying out of her head. 'It's probably just a bad bruise. I feel as though I've got one on my hip as well, and no, you're not going to check that out.'

He smiled briefly, appreciating what she was saying. Nevertheless his smoky eyes were grave. 'Lara, either I take you to the hospital, or I send for a doctor to confirm my opinion. Either way you'll end up there. So you may as well go with good grace.'

'You're making too much fuss,' she retorted.

'I don't think so.'

'And how would you know what I've done?' she asked sharply, feeling oddly irritated by his manner.

'Because I'm a dab hand at first aid. It's an essential skill when you're messing around with boats. Unexpected things can happen. Believe me, Lara, I'm not being paranoid.'

CHAPTER FIVE

THE X-ray confirmed that Lara had a fractured bone in her wrist and torn tendons, and by the time her arm was set in plaster it was too late to go back to Bryce's place. He took her home instead.

Helen was still out so Bryce settled her on a chair on the veranda and then busied himself making cheese and mushroom omelettes, something easy for Lara to manage one-handed. They ate them with French bread and sweet, juicy tomatoes picked from Lara's aunt's vine. Citronella candles kept the insects at bay and if it hadn't been for the pain throbbing through her arm Lara would have enjoyed this time spent with Bryce.

During the hours they'd sat waiting at the hospital he'd been like the true friend he'd said he wanted to be. There'd been no innuendoes, no advances, nothing to make her feel uneasy. If anything, she'd been the one who'd wanted more. Even now, in pain, she was so vitally aware of him it was unreal.

'Not quite the meal I'd planned,' he said with a rueful grimace as he topped up her wine.

But a delicious one all the same, she thought. 'I'm sorry I've ruined your evening. You'd gone to so much trouble, I feel awful.'

'Don't even think about it,' he warned. 'Most of what I've cooked will freeze. You'll have to come another day and help me eat it.'

'Not if it's something that needs a knife and fork,' she retorted quickly.

He gave a wicked, appreciative grin. 'I'd cut it up into dainty mouth-sized pieces and feed them to you one by one while I drown in your beautiful eyes.' He nodded to himself as if picturing the task. 'Yes,' he said gruffly, 'I'd enjoy that. It would be a good game.'

His pupils dilated as he looked at her and Lara's pulses fluttered. Trust Bryce to turn the situation to his advantage.

When the phone rang she asked him to answer it, and spent the time pondering about what the outcome of her relationship with Bryce would be. Of one thing she was certain: she couldn't pretend indifference for much longer. There had been a spark of attraction right from the beginning, which she'd wisely ignored, but it had grown dramatically, and she feared that any day now it would escalate until there was nothing either of them could do about it.

Although she hadn't known him long, Lara had begun to accept that Bryce was a man to be trusted. He wasn't all over her like a rash the way Roger had been. He was attracted to her, there was no doubt about that, but he respected her wishes and kept his feelings well-hidden, most of the time anyway, and she admired him for it.

'That was Helen.'

Lara looked at Bryce with a questioning lift to her brow. How handsome he was, how devastatingly sexy. Before they'd gone to the hospital he'd exchanged his towel for black linen trousers and a black polo-shirt and they suited him well, made him look earthy and mysterious and even more attractive, if that were possible.

'She isn't coming home tonight.'

Her mouth fell open; her heart stammered its amazement. 'Why not?'

'Something about unfinished business to be carried on over breakfast in the morning.'

Lara frowned. 'What business?' What was her aunt playing at?

'I've no idea,' answered Bryce with a wry grimace. 'But when I told her about your arm she was glad I'm here with you. She asked me to stay the night.'

Lara felt a swift explosion of fear. Bryce, here, in the same house, sleeping in the next bedroom. It didn't bear thinking about. Or was it anticipation, not fear, that was zinging through her veins like an out-of-control freight train? 'She asked, or you suggested?' she wanted to know, disturbed to hear how uncertain her voice sounded.

He gave a brief lift of his shoulders, a slow smile telling all. 'Does it matter?'

'I don't need you, Bryce.' She thrust the words firmly. 'I can manage perfectly well on my own.'

'Of course you can.' His voice was dangerously calm. 'But humour me, just in case.'

'I don't feel like humouring you.' She felt trapped. This time she truly had been manipulated and she didn't like it. In fact, she'd like to bet that her aunt was staying out deliberately. Maybe she'd rung to say she'd be late, and when Bryce answered and told her what had happened she'd decided not to pass up such a splendid opportunity.

'Too bad,' he said in a rasped voice, 'because I'm staying whether you like it or not.'

The companionship had gone. It was her fault, Lara knew, but really, why did her aunt and Bryce insist on trying to rule her life? Why couldn't they let her make up her own mind?

She finished her meal in wounded silence, aware that Bryce was watching her, brooding, thinking, probably plotting. He and her aunt had done plenty of that, and even though no one was to blame for her injured arm, they'd both been quick to take advantage. She was still feeling decidedly disgruntled when he stacked their plates. His voice deep and gruff he said, 'I'll put these in the dishwasher. Is there anything I can get you? More wine? Coffee?'

Lara shook her head. 'Nothing, thanks. What I'd really like is to be left in peace, but I don't suppose there's any chance of that?'

'Not a hope in hell,' he answered with a satisfied smirk. 'You need me, Lara, whether you realise it or not. I won't be a minute.'

Lara rested her head back on the chair and closed her eyes. There was no way out of this so she might as well make the best of a bad situation. The worst that could happen was that Bryce would try to take advantage. Except that he hadn't yet, so why should she imagine he would tonight?

It was herself she was afraid of, if she was honest; it was her own feelings that ran riot and imagined the two of them making love. Bryce would never do anything against her wishes.

She was perfectly safe.

'All done.' Bryce dropped into the chair beside her. 'You look tired, Lara. Do you want to go to bed?'

'I do feel weary,' she admitted. 'What with all that

swimming, and then sitting around in the hospital, it's taken its toll.'

'I'm tired, too, if the truth's known,' he admitted. 'I think we should both retire.' He shot a look at his watch. 'No wonder, it's getting on for midnight.' He stood up and held out his hand.

Triggers of panic worked their way through Lara's veins. 'I can manage.'

'I'm sure you can.' His smile was disarming. 'But I pride myself on being a gentleman.'

What could she say to that? There was no threat, no underlying implication. It would be cruel to refuse. So she held out her good hand and he helped her to her feet. He made sure doors and windows were locked before they walked side by side along the narrow corridor that took them to the bedrooms.

Helen's room was *en suite*; the other two shared a bathroom. Lara halted outside the second door. 'This is mine. Goodnight, Bryce. Thank you for looking after me.'

He looked as though he didn't want to let her go.

'I really will be all right,' she insisted.

'If you're sure?'

'Quite sure.'

He took her face between his palms and very lightly kissed her on the lips. It was a friendly kiss and yet it ignited Lara's senses to such an extent that she felt as if she was on fire. She swallowed hard and tried to pretend it hadn't affected her, but the way she scuttled into her room must have surely raised his suspicions.

She didn't care; he shouldn't have done that. Especially as they were alone in the house. Her cheeks flamed as she stood and listened for him to move on; only then was she able to relax.

But she hadn't realised how difficult it was to do things with one hand. The plaster came down almost to the tips of her fingers, rendering them useless. Trust it to be her right hand as well, she thought savagely. She gathered up her toiletries, listened carefully to make sure that Bryce was not using the bathroom, and then ran across the corridor like a scared cat, securely bolting the door behind her.

It took an age to brush her teeth and use the toilet. Everything was so unbelievably awkward. Back in her bedroom she attempted to undo the tiny buttons on her dress. It was hopeless. And the dress was too fitted to allow her to get it off without undoing them.

As if sensing her predicament Bryce tapped on the door. 'Are you managing?' he called. 'Can I be of any help?' Before she could even answer he pushed it open and stepped inside.

Bryce had wanted to undo those buttons from the word go. Anyone who designed a dress with buttons all the way down the front knew what they were doing. It was made to tease and tantalise, to send a man's imagination soaring and his testosterone levels sky-high. He'd guessed Lara would have difficulty undoing them and by the look of things he'd timed his entrance to perfection.

And she knew it!

Her horrified expression suggested that having him undress her was the last thing she wanted. Anyone would think he'd made a habit of harassing her. It hurt having her think this of him, but he didn't show it. She'd gone through a bad time; she still needed treating with kid gloves. He smiled gently, persuasively. 'Allow me.'

Lara inched nervously away and for a breathless second Bryce thought she was going to refuse. But then, as if silently telling herself that she would be safe in his hands, that if she didn't let him help she would have to sleep in her dress, Lara gave a hesitant smile. 'It's annoying, isn't it? I never realised how often you need to use two hands. There's so much I can't do.'

'I'm at your service, dear lady,' he replied with a mock bow.

'For six weeks, day in and day out?' she derided.

'If that is your wish, then I'll rearrange my schedule to—'

'Don't be silly, Bryce,' she cut in quickly. 'Aunt Helen will help. I wish she were here now.'

'You still don't trust me?' He kept his tone light but his heart was sad. He wasn't used to being held at arm's length, and it was especially hurtful when he loved her so much.

Loved her!

He almost reeled backwards with shock. How had that thought popped into his head? Did he love her? Could it be true? He thought a lot of her, yes. He desired her like mad, wanted to spend more and more time with her. But love?

Maybe, hopefully, it was because she was so unlike other girls. None of his previous girlfriends had made any attempt to hide their interest. Lara was different. He found her frustrating at times and yet something had made him continue to pursue her. Was that something love? Had it happened so suddenly that he wasn't aware of it?

'I do trust you, Bryce,' he heard Lara say as if from a distance. 'It's just that it's a little disconcerting to have to ask you to undo my dress.'

'You could pretend I am—your brother.' He'd seen the swift distaste in her eyes when she'd guessed what he'd been going to say and had quickly changed track. It made him wonder why he was bothering with her when she so clearly didn't want any kind of relationship. Except that there had been times when the blood had pumped as hotly through her beautiful body as it did his. She sent out confusing signals. He liked to think it was because she hadn't yet got over her husband's treatment of her, not that it was anything personal.

She gave a short laugh. 'I can't imagine any of my brothers doing that for me; they'd be too embarrassed. But, yes, I could do with your help. This has to be the worst dress I own to get on and off easily.'

Standing in front of Lara it took all Bryce's will-power not to pull her into his arms. She was so desirable, this lady, so essentially feminine, so lovely in every respect, how could he not love her?

The buttons were tiny, the buttonholes tight, his big fingers awkward. And his closeness to Lara didn't help. It was a severe test of concentration.

When the first buttons were undone, when he glimpsed the soft swell of her breasts and the delicate white lace of her bra, it was almost his undoing. He had the insanest urge to touch, to rip off her dress and expose everything instantly to his greedy eyes. It took every ounce of will-power to pretend he wasn't disturbed. And by the time he had undone enough buttons for the dress to slip down he couldn't pretend any longer, he couldn't even hold back.

He heard her say, 'Thank you, Bryce,' and he thought he heard a tremor in her voice as she clutched the dress to stop it falling altogether, but he knew he dared not look at her in case she saw the raging desire burning in his eyes. It consumed his whole body, made him unaccountable for his actions.

Of their own volition his fingers touched the provocative curves of her breasts, touched and stroked and adored. He couldn't drag his eyes away. It made his mouth run dry and his heart thunder. He felt like a teenager again experiencing his first love affair, slightly awkward, definitely hesitant, afraid of making a fool of himself.

But when she didn't push him away, Bryce bravely cupped her quivering breasts in his palms, allowing his eager thumbs to explore the tightly aroused buds. He couldn't help groaning; the sound escaped his throat like the cry of a wounded animal. When he heard Lara whimper too, he finally looked at her, and saw the same burning need in her eyes.

Unbelievably she made no attempt to push him away; rather her throat arched, causing her breasts to press deeper into his hands. It was his undoing. He couldn't help himself; he disposed of her bra in one swift, easy action and for a couple of seconds drank in the wonder of her nakedness. Her taut breasts with their delicate pink nipples were so beautiful, so perfect, so tempting, so utterly, utterly desirable.

Without even stopping to think whether she would reject him, whether he was going beyond the bounds of decency and whether it could spell the end of even a platonic relationship, he lowered his head and sucked first one nipple and then the other into his hungry mouth. It was like drinking the sweet nectar of life. She tasted and smelt like an exotic fruit. Nothing had prepared him for this moment. No other woman had excited him to such an extent.

And that was, he supposed, because he had never truly loved anyone else.

How he wished he could tell Lara of his love, but he couldn't. Not until she let go of her memories and accepted that he, Bryce, was different in every way. This moment was a rare one, circumstances perhaps making her grateful to him, allowing her to briefly drop her defences.

'You're so beautiful, Lara,' he muttered thickly against her breast. 'And I am so fortunate to have met you.'

Her reply was another whimper.

Encouraged, he let his teeth graze her nipples, was instantly excited by her jerk of pleasure and lifted his head to look into her glazed eyes, into her oh, so sexy eyes. Their colour had changed from cobalt to navy, her head was flung back, her lips parted. With a further agonised groan he feathered them with tiny kisses, pulled down her lower lip with a shaky thumb and kissed inside, stroked with his tongue, finally capturing her whole mouth.

When her tongue hesitantly and cautiously touched his he wondered if she knew what she was doing to him, how close he was to losing control? For so long he had wanted to kiss her, had been afraid she'd rebuff him, and now, unexpectedly, she was inviting him. Their tongues entwined, he explored and tasted and rejoiced, but at the back of his mind he knew that he mustn't go too far too soon or all would be lost again.

This was a special moment to be enjoyed and savoured, but he must take his lead from Lara, and already, as though she'd read his mind, she was gently withdrawing her mouth from his. But not, thankfully, her body. She rested her head on his shoulder and allowed him to hold her, and as he felt her soft and pliant against him it was as though they were two halves of a whole coming together, as though this was what had been missing from his life all these years.

He wondered if Lara felt the same.

But he knew it was time to call a halt. If he pressed her any further it would ruin everything. What headway he'd made would be crushed underfoot like freshly fallen snow. It would turn into something dark and nasty and she'd never let him close again.

And so, reluctantly, he let her go. He dropped his arms to his sides and took a step away from her. 'Can you manage now?' he asked gruffly, his voice still full of emotion.

Lara nodded, suddenly shy. Her dress had fallen to her ankles and all that protected her modesty was a pair of brief white panties. And amazingly she didn't try to hide any of her body from him; she stood there tall and proud, her breasts jutting enticingly. With iron control Bryce kept his eyes locked firmly into hers.

Lord, it was difficult, but he owed her that much at least. She'd allowed him well beyond her original boundaries and he dared not trespass any further without encouragement. 'I'll say goodnight, then. You know where I am if you need me. Just knock the wall.'

'I will,' she said quietly.

It was difficult keeping his eyes from straying, and a terrible struggle to walk to the door. He turned as he opened it, he couldn't help himself, it was an entirely involuntary reaction, and she was still standing exactly as he had left her. 'You are all right?' he queried, wondering if

she was in a state of shock, whether his kisses had trau-
matised her.

Lara nodded. Just go, she seemed to be saying, Let me
sort myself out; let me come to terms with what I've done.

He closed the door softly behind him and stood a few
moments in silence, gathering his racing thoughts together
but also listening. He was sure Lara could cope, but all
the same he wanted to be on hand in case she needed him.
As a teenager he'd broken his arm playing football so he
knew how inconvenient it could be.

At last he thought he heard faint sounds, as though she
was moving, getting ready for bed, probably slipping a
nightdress over her head, hiding her beautiful body. Even
thinking about those delicious curves sent his pulses racing
again, and with an angry, self-deprecating shake of his
head Bryce moved away and roughly pushed open the door
to the guest room.

Lara woke some time in the middle of the night and sat
bolt upright. There it was again. It sounded like someone
trying to break in. She let out a piercing scream and within
seconds Bryce banged her door open and leapt inside. He
snapped on the light. 'What's wrong?'

'I heard a noise like a door or window being rattled,
and then breaking glass.' It sounded pitiful now with the
light on, and if there had been anyone there she would
have frightened them away with her screams. But it had
been very real, and she was grateful that Bryce was here
with her, even if all he wore was a pair of black boxer
shorts. And what that hard-muscled body did to her was
best left unsaid.

Bryce laughed. 'That wasn't a burglar, it was me. I

couldn't sleep. I've been sitting out on the veranda with a shot of whisky. What you heard was me coming in. A gust of wind took the door out of my hand and in my rush to stop it banging and waking you I dropped the glass.'

Lara felt suddenly foolish and seeing her wry expression Bryce said quickly, 'You couldn't have known. And I shouldn't have been so clumsy. Helen's going to be cross with me for breaking one of her good glasses.'

Helen would never shout at Bryce, thought Lara. He was her blue-eyed boy, and would be even more of a favourite if he managed to persuade Lara to be his girlfriend. And judging by the way she'd responded to his kiss earlier it was much more of a possibility than it had been twenty-four hours ago.

It had taken her a long time to fall asleep after he'd left. To say she was confused was putting it mildly. What had happened to her good intentions? Why had she allowed him to touch her so intimately?

The answer was simple. She'd wanted him to. From the moment she'd had trouble unbuttoning her dress she'd had visions of Bryce doing exactly what he had done. She'd even imagined them making love, and if he'd pressed home his advantage she wouldn't have been able to stop him.

She wasn't in love, nothing like that, but he was a sensually exciting man and she was spiting herself by keeping him at arm's length. His touch, his kisses, had thrilled her to the very soul and she'd lain in bed aching for more.

'You're very quiet, Lara; you're not still shaken up?' A faint frown marred his brow.

Yes, I am. Not because of the noise, but because you keep arousing my base instincts. I want you in bed with me. I want you to make love to me. I want to feel you inside me. I want to torture your body the way you tortured mine.

What she actually said was, 'You woke me from a dream. I was walking along the shore watching the restless ocean. The beach was long and deserted and I walked and walked and I listened to the sound of the crashing waves. Then I realised there was another sound as well. I turned because I thought someone was following me. I thought it was pounding footsteps. But it wasn't; it was my heart. It was thumping so loud that it disturbed me. And then I heard breaking glass, and you know the rest.'

Bryce grimaced. 'It was probably me you heard walking up and down the veranda. I tried to be quiet but things have a habit of sounding much louder in the silence of the night.'

She wondered if it was because of her that he couldn't sleep. Whether he too had wanted to take things further. They had both lain in their beds wishing things were different, their bodies aching, their minds running in a thousand different directions at once.

But whereas she had fallen asleep Bryce had spent his time pacing the veranda. She knew what it was like to have sleepless nights; it had happened to her many, many times, and had she known what he was doing she would have suggested that he sit and talk to her. The hours were long with no company.

'Do you feel able to sleep now?' she asked, knowing that it would be impossible for her to drop off again.

'I've never been more wide awake. How about I make us both a hot drink? Could you manage that?'

Lara nodded. 'And I think I'd like to sit out on the veranda, too.'

And so they sat there on the swinging seat talking about anything and everything, and Lara felt comfortable in his presence. They watched the sky turn from inky black to pale grey and blue, then fire with colour as the sun began to rise. It was a spectacular time of day; it felt special and full of meaning, and Lara was glad she was sharing it with Bryce. It would live in her mind for ever. A new day, a new beginning, perhaps even the beginning of a new and more meaningful relationship.

It meant something to him too, she felt sure, because he took her hand and held it tight and she thought he was going to say something, but he didn't. And when he looked deep into her eyes and bowed his head towards hers, she thought he was going to kiss her, but he didn't do that either. Nevertheless it was an emotional moment, a special moment.

Finally he let go of her hand and stood up, saying thickly and urgently, 'I need a shower.'

To cool down his ardour? she wondered. Was he as aroused as she? 'Me, too,' she said, 'but I'm not supposed to get my plaster wet.'

'Then, we'll have to see what we can do about it. Stay there.'

He returned with a long, narrow plastic bag and an elastic band to hold it securely on her arm. 'Thank goodness Helen never throws anything away,' he announced triumphantly. 'Come along, you can go first.'

Surely he didn't mean that he was going to see her into the shower, watch over her, help her dress again afterwards? The thought triggered a myriad responses from nerve ends and pulses alike. It was like being pricked with a thousand needles all at the same time.

'I can manage on my own,' she said as he ushered her along the hallway, alarmed to hear her voice come out as a husky croak.

'I'm sure you can, but I'd like to be on hand just in case. Is that a problem?' He gave a wicked grin as he asked the question, knowing exactly what thoughts were going through her mind.

'I guess not.'

She managed to struggle out of her nightdress and wrap herself in a towel but it was an extreme effort, and really she ought not to be shy about asking Bryce for help. He was a man of honour and integrity; he would never attempt to touch her if he thought she was unhappy about it. In her mind that counted for a lot.

When she opened the bathroom door she found him hovering outside.

'Ready for your protective covering?'

'Mmm, yes.' Her blood seemed to boil as she let him fix the bag over her arm, but it was not until then that she wondered exactly how she was going to wash herself with her one good hand.

'You could do with some help, couldn't you?' he asked, reading her thoughts again.

Lara nodded.

'We could shower together. I promise to be a good boy.'

But could she promise to be a good girl?

CHAPTER SIX

'HELLO there, I'm home.' Helen's cheerful voice reached Lara and Bryce as they sat on the veranda, in shade now at this time of morning.

'We're out here,' Bryce called.

Lara looked at him and felt regret that their time alone was coming to an end.

Bryce too gave a rueful grin, easing his arm from around her shoulders before Helen breezed out to join them.

But her aunt was not fooled. She looked quickly from one to the other, saw the telltale expression on their faces, and gave a pleased smile. 'I'm sorry I left you in the lurch, Lara. What a good job Bryce was here when I phoned. How's your arm?'

'Good, thanks. It hardly hurts now.' Or was it because she had other things to take her mind off it?

Bryce sprang to his feet. 'Sit down, Helen; Lara's anxious to hear all that you've been up to. I'll go and fix a drink. What's it to be, coffee or lemonade?'

'Lemonade,' said Lara and Helen in unison.

'You look like the cat who's stolen the cream,' announced Helen as soon as Bryce was out of earshot. 'A good night, was it?' Her brows lifted, her mouth gave a cheeky smile.

'If you're asking whether I slept with Bryce, the answer is no,' Lara retorted. 'Stop letting your imagination run away with itself.'

'Something happened,' claimed Helen smugly. 'I'd need to be blind not to see the change in you two. But I won't pry; your business is your business.'

'Tell me, Aunt Helen,' said Lara drily, 'did you deliberately stay out last night?'

'Why would I do that, dear child?' Her face was a picture of innocence—too much innocence, Lara thought. 'It's as I told Bryce over the phone, my business meeting went on much later than expected.'

'What business meeting?' Lara asked bluntly.

'Shareholders,' answered Helen. 'I sold Tom's company when he died but I still have investments in it. I like to keep my eye on them.'

It sounded plausible, but Lara wasn't convinced. At least not about her aunt staying out overnight.

'It must have been some meeting to go on so long. And it's the first time I've known one to be held in the evening.'

Helen shrugged. 'We like it that way; it's more sociable. But dinner was delayed for some reason or other. Trouble in the kitchen, I believe. I didn't think you'd mind, especially when I found out that Bryce was with you. Of course I wouldn't have left you on your own knowing you were injured. I remember Bryce looking after me once when I sprained an ankle. He's superb in emergencies.'

Lara gave an inward smile. Her aunt's definition of superb would be very different to hers. He definitely wouldn't have helped Helen to shower. Why she had let him she didn't know, but it had turned into the most sensual experience of her life.

He had lathered her; she had lathered him. He had touched her in the most intimate of places; she had hesitantly at first and then more boldly touched him. They had ended up making love right there in the shower.

Her body gave a delicate shudder as she remembered her climax. Her whole body had been taken over by an intense, mind-blowing sensation. Wave after wave had engulfed her until she'd thought it was never going to stop. Nothing quite like it had ever happened to her before.

'You're right, Bryce is good in emergencies,' she agreed, deliberately pushing the thought out of her mind. 'I don't know what I'd have done without him.' Probably been as miserable as sin, unable to settle, and unable to do much for herself.

He returned with their lemonade and just looking at him in his sexy black tight-fitting trousers sent her heart into overdrive. He smiled as he placed her glass in front of her, a gentle, intimate smile that suggested secrets and happiness and more of the same to come.

Helen looked from one to the other but said nothing, though Lara didn't miss her nod of approval, and afterwards, when Bryce had left to do his day's work, her aunt said, 'I'm pleased to see you getting on so well at last. It's what I've hoped for ever since you came out here. I've never seen two people look more in love than you and Bryce.'

'In love?' echoed Lara. 'I wouldn't go that far.'

Helen pursed her lips and shook her head. 'Maybe you don't know it yet, or perhaps won't admit it, even to yourself, but believe me it's as clear as the nose on your face.'

Did she love him? Lara asked herself when Helen had gone indoors to change into something more comfortable. Was her aunt right? Or was it simply lust that she felt? He was handsome, he was fun, and he was certainly a magnificent lover. He'd taken her far beyond any bounds she'd reached before. But love? Commitment? Did she want to go that far?

And later that day when she had a phone call from Roger Lara knew she was right to be cautious. Roger had changed dramatically once they'd married and she had no proof that Bryce wouldn't do the same. She had friends too who complained that their husbands had changed, so it was best not to get too close, even though Bryce was a fantastic lover.

'Hi, Lara, it's me.'

'What do you want?'

'Now is that any way to greet your husband?'

'Ex-husband,' she reminded him tartly.

'Whatever. I need your help.'

'So I've heard. But if you've got yourself into trouble there's nothing I can say or do that will make any difference. And if that's why you've phoned me, then goodbye, Roger.'

'Wait, Lara,' he commanded urgently. 'You don't know the whole story.'

'I don't want to know,' she retorted bitterly. 'You're no longer a part of my life and my mother should never have told you where to find me.'

'Please, listen.'

Lara gave a mental shrug and remained silent.

'My new girlfriend's accused me of rape. She's taking me to court.'

So that's who it was, the new girl in his life. Bully for her. 'What do you want me to do about it?' she asked brusquely.

'I want you to give me a character reference.'

Lara only just stopped herself from laughing out loud. He'd done to this girl what he'd done to her, except that, whoever she was, she had more guts. Lara had thought that having a nice home and no money worries had made up for the way he'd treated her. How naïve, how utterly stupid she'd been. 'I can't do that, Roger. I know exactly how she's feeling. You did the same to me. And do you know what? I hope you're found guilty. Perhaps it will teach you a lesson.' And with that she slammed down the phone.

Afterwards she was trembling so much that her aunt poured her a brandy and insisted she drink it all up.

'He's a swine,' declared Lara vehemently.

'Of the tallest order,' agreed Helen once Lara had told her what it was about. 'You're well rid of him.'

'You don't think he'll bother me again?'

'If he does, he'll have me or Bryce to contend with. He sounds like a nasty piece of work. You were right not to agree to speak out for him.'

It was late evening before Bryce put in an appearance. Helen let him in and then conspicuously disappeared. Lara was bleary-eyed and thinking about bed, her almost sleepless night beginning to tell on her. In contrast Bryce looked as fresh as if he'd just got up: jaw shaven, hair brushed, eyes bright, crisp white shirt, pale blue chinos.

Her heart pounded simply looking at him.

'How are you?' he asked softly, lowering his head to chastely kiss her brow. 'How's your arm?'

'I'm well, and getting used to it, thank you.' She wanted to pull him down closer and offer her mouth; she wanted as much of this man as she could get.

'You look tired,' he said. 'Ought I to go?'

'No. I've been hoping you'd come.'

'Try keeping me away.' He grinned, flashing his even white teeth. 'I wish I could have made it earlier but I had lots to catch up on.'

'I kept you from your work,' she said sorrowfully.

'In the most pleasant of ways.'

'Sitting in hospital?' she asked with a raised brow.

'Even that had its merits. But I wasn't talking about that as you very well know. You've no misgivings, no regrets?'

Lara shook her head and her smile was wide. She couldn't seem to stop herself smiling. 'Have you?'

'I wouldn't be here if I had,' he declared softly, and this time he did kiss her. He sat beside her on the couch and took her mouth prisoner. Mindful of her arm he crushed her to him, and she heard the ragged thud of his heart echoing the unsteady beat of her own.

It was a long, never-ending kiss, arousing and exciting, revealing hunger and tension, whilst they both knew that somewhere Helen was hovering.

'I needed that,' he said thickly when he finally let her go.

'Me, too,' agreed Lara. It had given her a new lease of life. Sleep was now the furthest thought from her mind. 'How long can you stay?'

'As long as you want me.'

'You didn't have any sleep last night.'

'I don't need it.'

'Macho words,' she said with a laugh. 'You'll fall asleep on your next job. I think you should go.'

'When I've seen more of you.'

The innuendo sent a flush of heat through her veins,

made her wriggle in her seat. 'It's late, it's almost ten o'clock.'

'We could go to bed.'

'And shock Aunt Helen?'

'Would we?' he asked with a grin. 'She'd be delighted; she so wants us to get together.'

'I know.'

'She suspects?'

'Yes.'

'Then we have nothing to worry about.' And once more he kissed her; once more he aroused her to delicious heights so that she moved her body against his, showed by her every action that she was hungry for him again.

She was disappointed when Helen entered, but they didn't jump guiltily apart, neither of them seeing the point now. But her aunt's next words ruined the moment entirely. 'Have you told Bryce about Roger?'

Lara silently groaned. She didn't want to talk about her ex. They hadn't long and she wanted to savour her emotions; she wanted to go to bed still feeling Bryce holding and kissing her.

'Are you going back to him?' His voice was harsh, his eyes suddenly glacial.

'Of course not,' she protested. 'My mother had the story wrong.'

'He phoned Lara today. His girlfriend's accused him of rape,' announced Helen, unable to wait. 'He wants Lara to vouch for him in court.'

'I told him to get lost,' added Lara quickly before Bryce could jump to any more wrong conclusions.

His initial outrage swiftly changed to visible relief. 'Do

you think you've heard the last from him? Is he likely to ring again? If so I'll—'

Lara shook her head. 'I'm sure he got the message.'

Helen said, 'If he hasn't he'll have me to contend with. I won't have him upsetting Lara.'

'And if I'm here he'll certainly have a piece of my mind,' said Bryce strongly. 'Would you like me to go over there and sort him out?' He stood up, his fists clenched as he looked at Lara with concern deep in his eyes.

Lara felt flattered, but it was her own problem; she was the one who had to deal with it. 'That won't be necessary, either of you. I can handle him.'

'He has no right bothering you,' declared Bryce vehemently. 'I'd take great pleasure in telling him so to his face, following it up physically if necessary.'

'Now, Bryce.' It was Helen who spoke. 'Violence isn't the answer. Let's hope Lara's right and it's the last she hears from him.'

It seemed to be the case. There were no more phone calls. And in the days that followed Lara and Bryce spent as much time together as they could and sometimes he even managed to persuade her to stay overnight at his place. They were the happiest times.

Helen's friend's daughter arrived ready for her backpacking trip of a lifetime. Charlie Rowan—christened Charlotte, but a Charlotte she was not—was as thin and flat-chested as a boy. She had blonde hair cut unbecomingly short, a thin mouth and nose, and she would have been plain, except for her one redeeming feature—her beautiful green eyes. They had an almost luminous quality and people couldn't help but look into them.

Lara recognised her straight away as a girl who had

attended the same school as she had. She was several years younger than Lara, had been a bit of a tomboy, often in trouble, and had been known by everyone in the school for her wayward behaviour.

'It's a small world,' Charlie said as Helen introduced them, adding for Helen's benefit, 'We went to the same school.'

'What fun,' claimed Helen. 'I wasn't aware that you two knew each other. You'll have lots to talk about.'

Lara didn't particularly want to talk to Charlie. She'd never liked her and they had nothing in common. But she was polite for her aunt's sake.

That evening when Bryce came to pick her up she introduced him to Charlie. The younger girl took one look and couldn't keep her eyes off him. Not that Lara was surprised, because Bryce was totally gorgeous. A magnet for any female, young and old alike.

Fortunately Bryce didn't seem to notice. He took Lara to her now favourite seafood restaurant and he seemed a bit nervous, which was unlike him. At the end of the evening she found out why.

Looking into her eyes and lifting her one good hand he pressed it to his lips. 'Lara,' he said urgently, 'I know how you feel about committing yourself to another man but I can't be patient any longer. Will you do me the honour of becoming my wife?'

No words of love had been spoken between them so to say that Lara was taken aback was an understatement. They were getting there, she knew, but marriage? It was still too soon. She couldn't accept. Not yet. She wasn't ready.

Why aren't you ready? What's stopping you? asked a tiny voice inside her head.

I need more time.

Time for what?

To make sure he's the right man. A feeble excuse! She wouldn't find anyone more thoughtful or caring than Bryce. And she was already halfway in love with him. So what was wrong with her?

'I've blown it, haven't I?' Bryce's concerned voice reached into her thoughts. 'I'm sorry; forget I said anything. You're not ready to trust yet, are you? I understand. I shouldn't have rushed you. Except that where you're concerned patience doesn't come into it. I want you now, Lara, I want you in my bed every night, I want you beside me, I want—everything.'

'I'm sorry,' she whispered. 'I am getting there, truly. If you could just be patient a while longer.'

'Of course. Let's go.' But he didn't take her straight home. They walked around the harbour; they became a part of the night scene that was so magical. There were other lovers strolling, many dining alfresco; there was music playing, the moon gilding the water. One of the motor launches glided in, spilling its passengers after an evening of excellent food and entertainment. It was a place made for love and romance and she knew why he had chosen to propose here.

They were silent, each deep in their own thoughts. She slid her fingers into his and squeezed. 'I promise not to keep you waiting too long, Bryce.'

'I would never harm you, you know that? I'd never make you unhappy.'

Lara nodded. 'I can't help how I am. Once bitten, twice shy, isn't that what they say?'

'Something like that.'

'I hope I haven't spoilt things between us?' He was so quiet she was scared that she had frightened him off altogether.

He heaved a troubled sigh and turned her to face him, putting his hands on her shoulders and smiling wistfully. 'It's me who's ruined everything. I leapt in when I should have remained patient. Forgive me, Lara.'

'There's nothing to forgive.' She lifted her face to his and he kissed her. It was an urgent, hungry kiss, one full of passion and promise and it left her breathless, making her wonder why she was keeping this perfect man waiting. She didn't even know herself. Except that the time wasn't yet quite right. It was still too soon after her acrimonious divorce.

The next day Bryce didn't come to see her, nor did he phone—the first time this had happened since she'd broken her arm—and Lara began to fear that despite what he'd said he'd taken offence and had decided that he was better off without her.

The following morning Lara went on the train with Charlie into Sydney. They took the ferry to Manly but it was nothing like being with Bryce, not half so much fun. When Charlie went swimming Lara could only sit and watch, and she was glad when they got home and even happier still when Bryce came to see her, full of apologies for his absence.

'Work caught up with me, I'm afraid,' he said, his warm, possessive kiss instantly reassuring.

Lara's fears disappeared. 'Don't worry about it. I know

you're a busy man.' She led him into the family room where she and Charlie had been watching TV. Helen was out somewhere with one of her friends.

But when Charlie began to monopolise the conversation, asking Bryce all sorts of questions about Australia, advice on where she should go, the best places to stay, becoming more animated than she'd been all day, Lara's pleasure in Bryce's appearance began to disappear.

No matter how often she tried to change the conversation Charlie quickly veered it back. Bryce, to give him his due, constantly gave Lara intimate, reassuring smiles, lifting his eyebrows as if to say, Sorry, but what can I do about it without being rude? But it wasn't the same. Of course he couldn't ignore the other girl, Lara understood that, but there was a difference between friendly conversation and someone completely taking over.

When Charlie had exhausted the topic of backpacking she took a sip from her cola and eyed Lara narrowly from over the top of the can. 'Why did you and Roger get divorced?'

'Why does anyone?' asked Lara with a shrug of her slender shoulders, wondering why Charlie couldn't have asked this question when they were on their own. She didn't particularly want to talk about her broken marriage in front of Bryce. 'It didn't work out.'

Charlie smirked. 'From what I heard you married him for his money. What happened, did you spend it all? Was he of no further use to you?'

Lara felt herself flushing a dark, ashamed red and was unable to look at Bryce. 'I think what happened is nothing to do with you,' she said shortly.

She was aware that Bryce's eyes were on her and were

coldly paralysing. What sort of opinion was he forming now? Damn Charlie Rowan and her big mouth. She needed time alone with him to explain. It couldn't be done in front of this boyish girl who was taking great delight in her discomfiture.

'I would never marry for money unless I was in love as well,' claimed Charlie. 'I bet he hated you spending it. I bet that's why he chucked you out.'

'I think that's enough.' Bryce's tone was icy as he sprang to his feet. 'Lara's affairs are nothing to do with you, Charlie, or me, or anyone else for that matter.'

Charlie flinched and Lara began to feel grateful, until he added, 'It's time I went. I have an early start in the morning. Don't bother to see me to the door, I'll let myself out.' His eyes met hers briefly and distantly, but before Lara could get up he had spun around and gone.

'I'm sorry, didn't Bryce know?' asked Charlie innocently.

CHAPTER SEVEN

BRYCE was angry. Deeply, savagely, mind-threateningly angry.

He'd thought Lara was different, had convinced himself that she was far removed from any of the other girls he'd dated who's only interest had lain in what they could get out of him. Instead she, too, had been cleverly stringing him along.

When Charlie had said that Lara had married Roger for his money he'd thought she'd been joking, but one look at Lara's stricken face had told him that the other girl had been speaking the truth. It had devastated him and he couldn't imagine how he'd been taken in so completely.

She'd pretended innocence, oh, yes; she'd given no clue that she was aware of his wealth, playing the game perfectly, even going so far as to refuse to marry him, asking him to be patient a while longer.

Why? So that she could dig even deeper into his background, make extra sure that she wasn't making a mistake the second time around? Maybe Roger hadn't been rich enough. Maybe this time she'd set her sights a bit higher.

He drank his third whisky in as many minutes, tossing it down his throat as though it was water.

Helen must have told Lara the truth about him, even though he'd specifically asked her not to. And probably Charlie Rowan knew, too, otherwise why would she have made those sly comments? But at least he'd found out before it was too late.

He, who prided himself on being able to spot a fortune-seeker a mile off, had been taken in by a pretty face and a delicious body. He'd believed her hard-luck story, had even felt sorry for her. He shook his head repeatedly. How could he have been so foolish?

On arriving home he'd scorned the apartment above the boathouse, returning instead to his spacious tiered mansion. The loft held too many memories, memories of nights spent there with Lara in his arms, nights of hot lovemaking and long, satisfying hours lying in each other's arms, sometimes sleeping, sometimes talking, sometimes simply experiencing the joy of being together. He didn't think he could ever bear to go there again.

He downed another whisky before heading for the shower. He gasped as the cold water hit his shoulders, but it was what he needed. He needed to exorcise Lara from his body and mind.

Impossible!

He came out shivering but she was still uppermost in his thoughts. A few more whiskies were what was needed, he decided, taking the bottle through to his bedroom. A short time later he lay in a drunken stupor.

It was mid-morning before he awoke with a thumping head and a sad heart. Still in the boxer shorts he had slept in he took a pot of coffee out to the terrace. The black coffee matched his thoughts.

He really had thought that Lara was as open and honest as the day was long. She'd not given the slightest hint that her interest in him was mercenary. She had even said that she couldn't understand anyone living in a big house like this. What was the point of it? she'd asked. Why would anyone want to live in such a huge place? She'd loved the boathouse apartment; it was perfect, just the right size. How cleverly she'd thrown him off the scent.

If it hadn't been for Charlie Rowan he'd never have found out Lara's motives until they were married. It had been clever, that, initially turning him down, making him believe she wasn't yet ready to remarry. She must have been confident that he wouldn't wait long before asking her again.

Lord, how it hurt to realise he'd been well and truly duped. He'd fallen in love, had wanted to spend the rest of his life with her. In his mind they'd had a large family. They'd filled his house with love and laughter. She wouldn't have been able to say then that a big house was unnecessary.

'Damn!' he swore out loud, slamming his fist so hard on the table that his cup fell over and hot coffee spilled onto his leg. 'Damn!' he yelled again as he jumped up and this time the table went flying.

He strode to the pool and dived in, swimming several punishing lengths before hauling himself out and flopping face down on a canvas lounger. The exercise hadn't helped. His mind was still as angry and as muddled as before. Did he go and see Lara and have it out with her, or did he ignore her? Shut her out of his life for ever more? This was the safest, sanest solution, and yet—

'Bryce?'

He frowned as he heard his name tentatively called, clenched his fists when he recognised her voice. How the hell she'd got in, he didn't know, unless he hadn't closed the gates when he'd arrived home in such a filthy mood last night. But at least it solved his dilemma.

'Lara,' he acknowledged curtly, sitting up and straddling the sun lounger. God, she looked good. She wore white denim shorts that revealed the long length of her lightly tanned legs, topped with a loose yellow T-shirt. He could be mistaken, but he felt sure she was braless beneath it. To tease him? Probably. Or because she couldn't fasten her bra with her arm out of action?

He hated having to accept that this was the most likely reason and forced his eyes up to her face, seeing misery and uncertainty. But it meant nothing. She'd already proved what a consummate actress she was. It was best to remember that rather than be taken in again by her clever words and sexy body.

'We need to talk.' Her voice was soft, almost inaudible, and she couldn't quite meet his eyes.

'Do we?' he asked harshly. 'I think I heard enough last night to convince me that I've been wasting my time.' And yet still his male hormones sent his mind into a spin and his body into orbit. Damn! Why did she have to come today? Why couldn't she have waited until he'd got his thoughts in order? His head still ached, he hadn't brushed his teeth nor had he shaved; he felt rotten and out of sorts, and he wasn't even decently dressed. The last thing he wanted was a confrontation with Lara.

'I need to explain.' Her fingers twisted nervously together; she kept moving from foot to foot, and she was gnawing her bottom lip so fiercely that he felt sure she would draw blood. She had a canvas bag slung over one shoulder and it slipped off but she seemed not to notice, leaving it where it fell, her eyes now fixed pleadingly on his.

'I'll make some fresh coffee,' he said gruffly, heading indoors. He really didn't want her here but he could hardly send her away in the state she was in. He filled the kettle and reached down a cafetière, cleaned his teeth while he waited, and shrugged into a clean pair of shorts and a black vest.

When he rejoined her, Lara was sitting waiting, having righted the table he'd knocked over and attempted to clean up the mess. 'I didn't know you had free use of the house as well as the pool?' she said with a puzzled frown.

'Didn't you?' His tone was deeply sceptical, his eyes cold.

'Why should I?' She looked confused.

'I thought you knew all about me.'

'I do; I thought I did. You're confusing me, Bryce. What are you saying?'

More good acting. She'd missed her vocation, he thought angrily. 'Let's deal with the issue of you and Roger first,' he said in a rasping voice.

Lara winced, visibly uncomfortable.

'Charlie said you married for money. Is that right?'

She chewed her lip again, obviously weighing up how much to tell him.

'I think your silence is answer enough.' He thrust out the words fiercely, smoky eyes hard and unremitting.

'Actually, yes, I did,' she admitted finally. 'But it's not how it seems.'

'If you married for money and not love, then it's exactly how it seems.' His nostrils flared, mouth turning down at the corners, muscles jerking in his jaw, his whole body taut. 'You've let me down, Lara. I didn't think you were a mercenary little witch. I've been a fool, a damned, stupid fool.'

Lara flinched as he spat the words at her. 'You don't understand,' she protested. 'I had a tough childhood. I saw my mother go without so that she could feed and clothe us. I swore I'd never let the same to happen to me.'

'So instead of joining the lottery with the rest of the crowd and marrying for love you hedged your bets and chose a rich guy instead,' he said sneeringly. 'Did love ever come into the equation? Did you really think it would last?' He prayed she'd say yes; he wanted to be wrong; he didn't want to find her completely without morals. But her answer sent his hopes nosediving into his shoes.

'He was good-looking; he was interested in me; I thought I loved him.'

Was that a touch of defiance in her tone? 'You mean you took advantage of the fact that he fancied you.' He thrust the words at her. 'You had pound signs in your eyes when you decided that you were in love. Thank God I found out in time. I've had my fill of greedy, money-grabbing females.'

Lara frowned. 'What are you talking about?'

'As if you don't know,' he said, snarling. Lord, she was going to play it through to the bitter end. 'And if Charlie hadn't opened her mouth I might have continued to be taken in. I have something to be grateful to her for.'

'I still don't know what you're saying.'

Bryce sprang to his feet and almost knocked the table over again. Only Lara's lightning reaction saved the coffee pot from falling. He moved behind her, his hands on her shoulders, fingers digging so painfully into her soft skin that she winced, his head bowed so that his words hissed savagely into her ears. 'If you're trying to make out that you didn't know I was a wealthy man, that you didn't know I own this property, that you didn't know I run a whole fleet of cruisers down there on the harbour, then I suggest you change your tune, and quickly. Because I have great difficulty in believing that you're innocent.'

Lara froze, her mind unable to take in what he was saying. Helen would have told her; Bryce would have told her. What reason had either of them for keeping such a secret?

'Have you nothing to say?'

Still his fingers paralysed her; his voice was harsh and condemning in her ears. Lara shuddered. 'Is it true?' she whispered. She had never known Bryce like this; it was a side of him she hadn't suspected and didn't much like.

'Of course it's damn well true, and you know it.'

'I don't, I didn't, I never—'

'Never what? Thought I'd guess what your little game was?' he said, sneeringly. 'What puzzles me is why you turned down my offer of marriage. Or was that another of your little tricks to put me off the scent? Very clever! The next time I proposed it would have been a swift, Yes, please, I suppose.'

Lara had taken enough. She leapt up and spun around to face him, eyes glittering with fury and contempt, whilst still acknowledging that even in his anger he remained hugely attractive. 'Has it ever occurred to you that you might have this all wrong?'

Brows rose almost to his hairline. 'Oh, yes, it's occurred to me, lady, but only for a very brief second. The evidence is before me. Leopards never change their spots. What you've done once, you'll do again. Do you know what? I'm almost feeling sorry for good old rich Roger. Was Charlie right, did he come to his senses and kick you out?'

'Damn you!' Lara flung the words furiously. 'Damn you to hell! And the next time you think someone's after your precious money then get your facts right before you make accusations.' With a resentful flash of her cobalt eyes she tossed her head and started to march back the way she had come.

How she was going to get home Lara had no idea. She'd asked the taxi driver to wait five minutes in case Bryce wasn't in, but he'd have long gone by now. There was no way she was staying here to face insult upon insult, though. Unfounded ones at that.

The fact that Bryce was a millionaire—he'd have to be to live in a place like this, maybe even a multimillionaire if he ran a lucrative business—had blown her mind. He'd given her no clue; nothing had prepared her; the shock was like a bolt from the blue. She could see why he'd leapt to conclusions when Charlie had asked her sly questions but he could at least have given her the benefit of the doubt, talked things over instead of firing the bullets first. *And more importantly, why the hell hadn't he told her?* Why had he kept a secret as well?

As the thought flashed into her mind Lara halted in her tracks. She swung around, eyes bright with accusation, and put the question to him. 'You talk about me not being honest, why don't you take a long, hard look at yourself? If I've been guilty of withholding facts, then so have you.'

'With very good reason,' he answered coolly. 'Since my business took off I've been a target for women like you.'

'And so the little charade about being an odd-job man

was a test?' He'd convincingly explained away the expensive restaurants, his use of the pool. Nothing had prepared her for this moment. 'I suppose you told Aunt Helen to say nothing either?'

He shook his head in savage frustration. 'Does it matter what I said to Helen? The truth's out. I know now what sort of a person you are.'

'You know what I was…' she thrust the words at him furiously, '…not what I am. I made a mistake and I freely admit it. And if you're so interested in knowing the truth, then think about this. If I'd known you were a rich man I wouldn't have so much as looked at you.' Let alone have fallen in love with him! 'I've had my fill of men and their money. They're conceited bigots with huge chips on their shoulders. So if you think you've had a close shave, then think again, buddy, because so have I.'

This time she walked away and didn't look back.

This time it was Bryce who called her.

'Lara.'

She ignored him.

'Lara.'

'Goodbye, Bryce,' she called over her shoulder.

But when she reached the iron gates they wouldn't open. He'd electronically armed them, effectively making her his prisoner until he decided otherwise. Though what more there was to say she had no idea.

She turned, and with her back to the gates watched as he walked towards her. There was still no denying that he was gorgeously handsome. His black vest revealed the tautness of muscles, the power that lay beneath the golden skin. He was as lean as a panther, walked with the same lithe grace, and was equally dangerous.

By the time he reached her Lara's heart was racing painfully. Eyes met eyes; eyes locked and waited, his icy cold and dangerous, hers, she imagined, far too revealing. In fact her whole body felt dangerously close to meltdown. Despite his anger, or possibly because of it, she felt a pulsing, animal hunger deeper than ever before. Her breathing grew shallow, her breasts visibly rising and falling, peaking nipples pushing against her soft cotton top.

Bryce's fingers were flexing, his nostrils flared. He'd like nothing more than to lash out at me, thought Lara worriedly, and there was no one here to protect her. It was just the two of them. She had walked straight into his trap.

'There's one more thing I want to do before I banish you from my life,' he growled out, pushing his face up close to hers. 'I want to remind myself what it's like to kiss a scheming, avaricious, hussy.'

Lara closed her eyes, wincing inwardly. Did she take this, or did she follow her instincts? Instinct won. Her hand came up and before he could guess her intentions she struck him hard across the face.

He staggered backwards, at least that was what she wanted to think. Actually he simply stepped back, his eyes shocked, and she watched in fascination as his cheek went first white, showing the exact imprint of her hand, each finger incredibly outlined, and then red as the blood rushed to the surface.

She wasn't sorry; he'd deserved it. He was a mean-minded swine intent only on her destruction. 'You asked for that,' she said in a tone deliberately devoid of emotion. 'Now open this gate and let me go.'

'Not until I do what I set out to do.'

'Go to hell,' she snapped.

'I'm already there.' And before she could stop him, before she could even move, he had bounced into action, strong arms snapping around her, heedless of her injured arm, his mouth moving at lightning speed towards hers.

It was a kiss designed to humiliate, a kiss that savaged her mouth, a kiss that demanded compliance.

It was also a kiss that sent a message to the very core of her, a message that suggested she respond, a kiss that told her she was undoubtedly in love with him.

I can't kiss him!

But you want to, insisted an inner voice.

It wouldn't be right, she answered.

Why not?

He hates me now; he's punishing me.

But you're enjoying it.

So?

Enjoy it!

But Lara couldn't. Although it aroused every one of her base instincts she couldn't relax, couldn't respond. She couldn't move her body against his in delightful anticipation. Because that was what he wanted her to do, what he hoped for, what he expected.

He wanted proof that she would try to snare him no matter what. He expected her to flaunt her body sexily against him, arousing him to such a pitch that he would be prepared to forgive her anything.

In your dreams, she thought, seething silently. He was getting nothing from her. If he wanted to believe the worst, then let him. It proved he wasn't half the man she'd thought and she was well rid of him. In her eyes, his deception was far worse, and yet he was laying the blame on her.

When his hand lifted her T-shirt and squeezed her breast, hurting and yet exciting at the same time, she did her best to ignore it. And when he lowered his head and sucked her nipple into his mouth, teeth grazing and nipping, it was hard to stop herself from crying out. Not with pain, but pleasure.

Pleasure at a time like this? Her whole body was pulsating to some ancient erotic rhythm. It would be so easy to go with the flow. It was with a cry of sheer desperation that she wrenched free, her eyes a glazed, angry blue, her limbs trembling so violently that she was afraid she would collapse in an undignified heap.

'Had enough?' he jeered.

'Shouldn't I be asking you that question?' She thrust the words back. 'Open the gates, damn you, and let me go!'

His mouth was soft and moist from kissing her, but it was the only gentle part about him. His eyes still condemned, the skin on his face was pulled taut over rigid bones, his body was angular and stiff like a robot who'd run out of steam. He pulled a black remote from his pocket.

'Go!' he commanded as the gates swung slowly and silently open.

To your doom, he seemed to be saying.

And they closed with an ominous clunk behind her.

Aunt Helen, when she found out what had happened, was distraught. 'It can't be,' she protested in very real anguish. 'I'll have a word with Bryce. There's been some misunderstanding.'

'Please don't,' implored Lara. 'It's over between us. I don't think our relationship ever really got off the ground.'

'That was only because you didn't want it to,' Helen

pointed out significantly. She laid her hand gently on Lara's arm. They were sitting out on the veranda, Charlie having gone into Sydney to meet some other backpackers with whom she planned to travel, and they were quietly getting through a bottle of Helen's home-made wine. 'Is it really true that you set your sights on Roger because he was wealthy?'

Lara pulled a rueful face. 'I'm afraid so. It became a standing joke at school because I was always saying I'd marry a rich man. We got taunted, my brothers and I, because we wore second-hand clothes. I didn't want to put my own children through that. It seemed a simple solution.'

'Then you discovered that money doesn't always bring happiness? Did you tell Bryce what happened?'

'Some,' she admitted. 'Not the real reason I married. I wish you'd explained about his money, though. I wouldn't have looked at him twice.'

'I'm sorry,' said Helen with an apologetic smile. 'I couldn't let him down when he asked me not to. I didn't think it would matter; I thought it would be a wonderful surprise.'

'It's hard to take in,' said Lara, shaking her head. 'You both had me convinced that he pottered around helping people. I thought he was a good, honest, hard-working, generous man.'

'Which he is,' insisted Helen, swallowing the last of her wine. 'Every one of those things. Despite running a highly profitable and successful business he still has time to give to other people. Bryce Kellerman is one of a kind.'

It was obvious her aunt had never seen the side of him that he'd shown Lara this morning. There had been nothing generous about him then. He'd formed an opinion and had stuck to it. It had been like being in a witness box. 'Did you marry this man for his money?'

'Well, I—'

'Please answer, yes or no.'

Bryce hadn't wanted explanations; he'd been brutally obnoxious, proving beyond any shadow of doubt that he'd never felt any real affection for her.

And what that last kiss had been about she'd no idea. If it had been intended to degrade, then he'd succeeded. She'd walked away feeling thoroughly soiled, and as though she'd had lead in both her heart and her shoes. It had been an effort to put one foot in front of the other and it had taken an age to reach the nearby town where she'd found a taxi to take her back to her aunt's.

'I think I ought to invite Bryce to dinner one evening. It's obvious that you both need to talk.'

Lara closed her eyes for a second, her hair flying as she vigorously shook her head. 'Don't even think about it. I tried talking; it didn't work.'

'It might when he's had time to come to terms with what he's found out,' said her aunt calmly. 'You can't blame him for thinking the worst. He's had some bad experiences with so-called social climbers. We'll give him a few days and then—'

'I'd rather you didn't,' insisted Lara, while knowing at the same time that Bryce was her aunt's friend and if she wanted to invite him there was nothing she could do about it.

When Charlie came home later she ignored their gloomy faces and said cheerfully, 'No Bryce this evening? What a pity, I wanted to say goodbye. I'm off on my travels tomorrow.'

Now that she'd effectively ruined her relationship, thought Lara resentfully. Why couldn't she have kept her mouth shut? Actually she was surprised that Charlie was leaving already. She'd assumed that the reason Charlie had informed on her was because she fancied Bryce herself.

'I thought you'd be here for days yet,' said Helen, unconsciously echoing her thoughts.

Charlie grinned. 'So did I until I met Claire and Jaz and the others. It's going to be fun.'

Yes, she'd be having a ball, thought Lara. She'd not give a second thought to the fact that she'd ruined Lara's life. Or was that being a bit extreme? Her life wasn't exactly ruined, was it?

If she'd truly loved Bryce she'd have agreed to marry him, wouldn't she? It wasn't love that she felt, simply desire for a very sexy male animal. Thank goodness she'd found out in time the darker side of his character.

Perhaps she ought to leave, too. Though where would she go? She wasn't ready yet to return to England. Maybe she could also do a bit of backpacking? Or find a temporary job and a room to stay in. That way Helen could have Bryce over as often as she liked.

In the days that followed Helen did her best to persuade Lara to contact Bryce, but as far as Lara was concerned there was no point. If he chose to believe the worst there was nothing more she could do about it.

When he did pay a visit Lara was out. She'd gone to the Imax in Sydney to see one of their brilliant three-dimensional films on the larger than large screen, having lunch afterwards at a sandwich bar overlooking the harbour, and generally reminding herself of the times she'd spent there with Bryce. There were good memories here, happy memories, memories that would live in her mind for ever.

She watched the ferries and the cruisers frequently crossing the waters and wondered which ones were his. She studied the names. The most likely one was Kayman Cruises. The initial of his surname plus the last three letters? Could that be it?

They were very smart in white with a blue trim, symbols representing ocean waves beneath the name. She walked across and studied the advertising board. Maybe she'd book herself on one of their cruises. An afternoon-tea cruise perhaps. Or lunch one of the days. Not dinner, not on her own.

She wanted to ask whether this was indeed Bryce Kellerman's cruise line, but the boat sitting in the water was locked and empty—another couple of hours before it departed. She decided not to wait.

When she got home Helen told her that Bryce had called round. 'I tried to talk some sense into him,' she said unhappily, 'but it didn't work. I have to confess, I've never known him so stubborn.'

'I've told you, it's over,' declared Lara, thinking how pale and distressed her aunt looked. 'There's nothing you can do.'

'But you're so right for each other.'

'That's your opinion,' said Lara softly. 'Dear aunt, you don't look well. Why don't you lie down?'

'I don't want to lie down,' Helen snapped. 'I want you two to see sense. What's the point in you both being unhappy? Sort yourselves out, for pity's sake.'

Lara had never seen her aunt this upset and angry. It was so out of character. And it was all her fault! 'I'll make you a cup of camomile tea,' she offered gently.

'Forget the tea,' retorted her aunt. 'If you want to do something useful, go and see Bryce.'

Lara was getting nowhere. Perhaps best to go to her room and give her aunt time to calm down. 'I'm sorry,' she said, 'but I can't do that. I'm going to take a shower.' But she hadn't even reached the bathroom when she heard her aunt call out.

By the time Lara reached her, Helen was unconscious on the floor.

CHAPTER EIGHT

APPARENTLY Helen's heart condition had first shown itself when her husband had died, but since then she'd had no further problems, not real problems.

Until now!

Lara blamed herself entirely.

She was willing to bet that Bryce didn't know either. Nor did her mother, or she'd surely have said.

The ride to the hospital in the ambulance had been worrying. Her aunt had lain still and lifeless, wired up to a machine, and the hours waiting around afterwards had been the longest of Lara's life.

Finally, much to her relief, Helen was pronounced out of danger, though they planned to keep her in for further tests and monitoring. Lara took a taxi home eventually, and was stopped on the doorstep by an elderly neighbour.

'I saw the ambulance,' she said. 'Whatever's wrong?'

And when Lara told her, Mary was distraught. 'Poor Helen. She's always been so good to me. Tell her I'm thinking of her. Is there anything I can do to help?'

'There's nothing you can do for my aunt,' said Lara. 'But I'd be grateful of some help myself. This darned arm is such a nuisance.'

Lara was back again at the hospital first thing the next morning.

Her aunt looked much better, some colour having returned to her face, though her every pulse and heartbeat was still being carefully checked. She smiled wanly at Lara. 'Silly me, letting that happen.'

Lara fondly kissed her cool cheek. 'It's my fault. If I'd known I would never have—'

'How could you be expected to know when I told no one?' interrupted Helen. 'Who wants to be lumbered with someone else's problems? Have you rang Bryce?'

Lara shook her head as she sat down beside the bed.

'I'd like you to.'

'I'll do it when I get home.'

'Good.' Helen closed her eyes, as though even this short conversation was too much for her.

'Would you like to get some sleep?'

'Sleep? In this place?' Helen smiled faintly. 'It's impossible! They tell you to sleep then just as you drop off they come to check your blood pressure or your temperature or whatever else takes their fancy. You could go and ring Bryce now, though, catch him before he goes to work.'

'I don't have his number.'

'Nor can I remember it for the moment,' said Helen, rubbing her brow. 'Try directory service.'

When she heard Bryce's voice, Lara's knees turned to jelly and it was all she could do to speak. 'It's Lara,' she managed hoarsely.

A moment's telling silence, then a roar. 'Go to hell,' he snarled before the line went dead.

If she hadn't known before that he wanted nothing more to do with her, then she most definitely did now. It was not a nice feeling. Lara dialled again, her heart slamming against her ribcage. He was making this incredibly difficult.

The phone rang six times and his answering machine came on. 'You've reached Bryce Kellerman. Leave a message and I'll get back to you a.s.a.p.'

So he thought he'd get rid of her that way! Lara felt her blood rising. 'I know you're there, Bryce,' she yelled. 'Pick up the damn phone. I'm not ringing for myself, it's Helen, she's—'

'Helen?' His voice rang loud in her ear. 'What's wrong?'

'She's in hospital.'

'What the hell for? What's happened to her?'

'She's had a heart attack.'

'I'll be there.' The line went dead so suddenly that he must have been slamming it down even as he spoke, and in almost no time at all he marched into the ward. He'd gone through every red light on the way, decided Lara.

He ignored her, looking directly at Helen, bending low over her, kissing her, holding her hand. 'What have you been up to?' he asked gently.

Helen smiled into her dear friend's face. 'How good of you to come so quickly.'

'You haven't answered my question. You don't get a heart attack for nothing.'

'I've always been prone to them.'

'Since when? Not in all the years I've known you.'

'My first was when Tom died.'

'And since?'

'None,' she answered sheepishly.

'So what brought this on?' He turned and looked accusingly at Lara as he spoke.

'How do I know?' asked Helen. 'It's just one of those things. Don't let's talk about it.'

'I think I'll go home,' said Lara to her aunt. 'I'll come back later.' *When you're alone,* she added silently.

It was mid-afternoon when she returned and Bryce was still sitting beside the bed. Helen was asleep.

'I'd like a word with you,' he said in a rasping voice, warning Lara that he'd been waiting for her.

He'd evidently wheedled out of Helen the reason for her heart attack and now, judging by the ominous glint in his eyes, he was going to tell her off.

Lara figuratively squared her shoulders as she followed him from the room. They went outside into the crippling heat of the day, where searing blue skies and a red-hot sun made life uncomfortable. Perhaps that was what he wanted, to add to her discomfiture. Lara turned and faced him, her cobalt eyes belligerent, her chin high. 'So what is it you want to say?' Her heart pumped painfully fast and there was no ignoring the fact that he still had the power to assault her senses. It was a dismaying thought. She would like to be able to say that she was well and truly over him.

He shoved his hands into his trouser pockets and frowned down at her. 'I'm worried about Helen.'

'So am I,' she retorted wishing he hadn't done that. His trousers stretched taut across lean hips, reminding her of his hard, exciting body, drumming up all sorts of unwanted images.

'It's upsetting her that we've had a difference of opinion.'

To put it mildly, thought Lara.

'And, although it's impossible for us to get back on the same footing, I think, for Helen's sake, that we should at least make a pretence of being friends.'

Lara swallowed hard. This wasn't what she'd expected. And they'd tried this before. Look where it had got her.

'Do you agree?'

'Er, yes.' Though Lord knew how she'd manage it when every nerve end sizzled at the mere sight of him. It wouldn't be easy to pretend immunity; in fact it would be downright impossible.

He frowned. 'You don't sound very convinced.'

She simply couldn't drag her eyes away from the front of his trousers, the way they... 'Of course I am.' She gulped guiltily, 'Helen must be reassured.'

'She'd set her heart on us becoming a real couple.'

'I know.'

His lips tightened and Lara wondered whether he'd guessed at the dangerously sexy thoughts flitting through her mind? Or did he think she wasn't being suitably concerned?

'So I think it's very important that she believes we've patched up our differences. At least until she's home and feeling well again. After that, well, we'll have to let her down gently.'

Lara nodded.

'I know it will be difficult—for both of us.'

'Extremely so.'

'Dammit, Lara, what the hell is going through that mind of yours?' He grasped her shoulders and forced her to look at him. 'This is as difficult for me as it is for you, but I'm damned if I'm going to let our personal disagreements ruin Helen's health.'

'I don't want that either,' she agreed, shaking off the image of his sexy body, concentrating at last on what he was saying. 'I love my aunt dearly; I want her to be well again; I don't want to have to feel guilty for the rest of my life because something I've said or done causes a fatal heart attack.'

'Precisely,' he snapped. 'Keep that in mind. Let's rejoin her.'

Outside the door to her private room Bryce stopped and faced Lara. 'We need to make this convincing.' His hands cupped her face, his head swooped and his mouth possessed hers in a kiss that sent her mind reeling.

Did he have to kiss her so deeply? Lara agonised, as his tongue invaded and excited. Her aunt didn't need to be *that* convinced, surely? The kiss went on and on and in the end Lara couldn't contain her feelings. She convulsively wriggled her hips against him, discovering to her horror that he was equally aroused.

She struggled away from him, her heart thudding, her skin on fire. 'Was that really necessary?' she asked furiously.

'I think so. Helen will have no trouble now in believing that we've made up. You look truly sparkling.' Before she could make any kind of retort he took her hand and dragged her into the room.

Helen took one look at their faces and beamed. 'Tell me I'm not seeing things?'

'You're not seeing things,' declared Bryce, his smile as wide as hers. 'We've come to our senses.' And he prayed Helen would believe him. He'd had a very enlightening conversation with her yesterday.

Helen looked from him to Lara who nodded her agreement. 'We're in love,' she said simply.

That shook him. Love was the furthest thought from his

mind. Helen had apparently, despite his suspicions, not said a word to her niece about what he really did for a living. Which meant that Lara had actually turned him down because she thought he *hadn't* any money. Exactly the opposite of what he'd thought when he'd found out why she'd married her first husband. Dammit! He'd been such a fool. *'We're in love.'* She'd said it so easily, so convincingly. Bryce shuddered as he thought of the near miss he'd had.

'I'm so happy,' said Helen, her eyes filling with tears as she held out her hands to both of them.

When they left the hospital Helen was sleeping, a contented smile on her lips. 'I don't think it will be long now before she's home,' said Bryce as they walked to their respective cars.

Lara nodded. 'I'm glad you suggested we make up. It seems to have done the trick. I felt so guilty.' There was a feverish light in her eyes as she looked at him and Bryce heeded the warning inside his head.

'This isn't permanent,' he snarled. 'I haven't changed my mind about anything. You'd do as well to remember that.'

Lara's head rocked back as though he had struck her, her blue eyes sparking resentment and aggression. 'How the hell am I supposed to be nice to you when you speak to me like that? Either you want me to be friendly or you don't. Which is it? I can't turn it on and off at will. I'm not a good enough actress.'

Reluctantly he accepted that she was right, they couldn't continually switch moods; it had to be all or nothing. And maybe the all thing wouldn't be so bad. Her beautiful body still had the power to arouse every base instinct he possessed. Why not take full advantage? It was no less than she deserved.

'In that case, have you plans for tonight?' Simply looking at her created havoc with his hormones.

Lara's eyes widened, making him think of blue waters lapping against his hot body, beckoning and arousing, making him want to dive into them, and he was shocked to feel disappointment when she said primly, 'I don't think we need go that far.'

'I was suggesting nothing but a meal,' he retorted, squashing his errant thoughts. 'Why should we eat alone?'

'Because I'd prefer it,' she retorted. 'Goodbye, Bryce.'

He inclined his head in acknowledgement, angry with himself now. 'I'll see you at the hospital tomorrow?'

'Don't you have other more important things to do?' she asked scathingly. 'Like running a business?'

He smiled briefly, grimly. 'It's in the capable hands of Gloria, my manager. There's not much that girl can't do.' He caught the flicker of surprise on Lara's face and guessed she was wondering whether he had any sort of relationship going with Gloria. He found it highly amusing and injected a note of pleasurable softness into his voice. 'She phones me every night with a run-down on the day's events. I don't know what I'd do without her.'

'You could take your responsibilities seriously instead of pretending to be who you're not.' Lara tossed the words at him, her eyes sparking fire.

He was glad she had reminded him of the reason she'd turned him down because he was in grave danger of losing his head over this exciting girl with the beautiful body. 'I'm not the only one who withheld the truth,' he cautioned coolly. 'Perhaps you're right, though, we shouldn't spend too much time together.' And with that he walked away.

Lara found the evening incredibly lonely. Mary had cooked her a meal but she didn't feel like eating it. It was all very well agreeing to a truce, pretending for her aunt's sake, but had Bryce any idea how hard it was for her? And as for asking her to join him for a meal, how insensitive could he get? There was only so much a girl could do, and spending a whole evening with a man who had made it clear he distrusted and despised her was not one of them.

Not surprisingly she couldn't sleep. Bryce was too much on her mind. He tormented her soul and her heart and she wondered if she would ever get over him.

She had taken to wearing skirts with elasticated waistbands and tops that she could pull over her head one-handed. Bras were a thing of the past: there was no way she could fasten them.

She dressed all in blue the next morning and when she went to the hospital Bryce was already there. He looked pleased to see her, smiling widely as he leapt up from his chair. He folded her in his arms and kissed her soundly and it was hard to remind herself that it was all for her aunt's benefit.

She looked down at Helen over his shoulder and saw her aunt smiling and nodding. She looked a hundred times better than yesterday. It was worth the pretence. Except that she wasn't pretending when her blood sizzled and her heart tried to catapult out of her chest.

'Bryce couldn't wait for you to arrive,' said Helen once they were both sitting at her bedside, hands linked like lovers unwilling to part. 'He's been like a cat on hot bricks.

I can't tell you how pleased I am that you've resolved your differences.'

'We're pleased, too, aren't we, darling?' Bryce looked lovingly into her eyes and Lara nearly fell off the chair. Had he no idea that if he carried on like this it would be twice as hard to walk away once she had served her purpose? Or was that his intention? Was this his way of punishing her? Did he know he could still arouse her with a look or a touch?

She smiled and nodded, unable to put the lie into words. 'When are they going to let you come home, Helen?'

'Maybe tomorrow,' her aunt replied. 'They're awaiting the results of some more tests. I can't wait to get out of here.'

And Lara couldn't wait either because then there'd be less chance of her seeing so much of Bryce. He'd call to see her aunt, yes, but, she'd be able to keep out of his way. As things stood he seemed prepared to spend all day and every day here. Gloria-whoever-she-was must be worth her weight in gold. It sounded as though she was running the company. A definite treasure. Was she also a part of his private life? Lara was amazed how jealous she felt. Was the woman in love with him? Were they having an affair? Did she know that he'd asked Lara to marry him?

It shouldn't really matter; Bryce could do as he liked, go out with whom he liked, bed whom he liked; it was nothing to do with her any longer. But the unhappy thought remained.

An hour later Bryce left, announcing that he'd be back again to take her out for lunch.

'There's no need,' Lara protested. 'I'll get a sandwich in the cafeteria.'

Before he could reply, Helen spoke for him. 'Of course you must go, Lara. It's depressing here. Enjoy yourself. I'll probably take a nap after lunch anyway, so it's the perfect opportunity for you two to spend some time together.'

Lara had no choice. She grimaced and shrugged. 'If you're sure.'

But she didn't enjoy her lunch. She was too aware of Bryce for comfort, aware of his eyes on her jutting nipples, feeling as though he was mentally undressing her. She answered his questions in monosyllables, toying with her food, wishing herself a million miles away. How was she going to live without this gorgeous man in her life? If only she'd told him the truth in the beginning. She could have made a joke of it, reassured him that money was no longer of any importance to her. And maybe he'd have told her the truth as well.

'This isn't going to convince your aunt.'

'What isn't?'

'Behaving as though I'm an obnoxious stranger. You were the one who said you couldn't turn your behaviour on and off.'

'I was wrong,' she admitted. 'I can't do this, Bryce; it's impossible.'

Eyebrows rose. 'You want Helen to have another heart attack? Are you forgetting how much she's set her mind on us becoming a real couple?'

'Of course I haven't forgotten,' she replied smartly, 'but you're going over-the-top. When I arrived this morning I thought you were going to eat me. Was it really necessary to be so enthusiastic?'

He gave a wicked smile. 'Helen loved it. And I think

you did, too. Or was that brilliant acting when your heart went into overdrive? When your body grew so hot I thought it was going to melt? Tell me I was mistaken.'

Lara couldn't lie. More heat suffused her cheeks. 'There're some things a girl can't help.'

'So you *can* run hot and cold, is that what you're telling me?' His smoky eyes were unwavering on hers, questioning, waiting.

Lara shrugged. 'I suppose so.'

'Suppose? You don't know?'

'What the hell is all this about?' Lara suddenly realised that she had raised her voice and people were looking at them. 'Why are you taunting me?' she asked urgently. 'Why don't you leave me alone?'

'Because, to be brutally honest, you intrigue me,' Bryce answered, picking up his coffee cup and swirling the contents around before finishing it off. 'You fancy me like hell yet try to pretend you want nothing to do with me.' His eyes were unwavering on hers.

'I do not fancy you,' denied Lara, a sudden, embarrassing heat invading her skin. Is that what he thought? 'It's only when you—well—when you kiss me. It's something I can't help. You're—good at it.' He inflamed her to depths unimaginable. 'But don't flatter yourself that I'm still interested because I'm not. I'll never again marry a rich man.'

Bryce raised a disbelieving brow before glancing at his watch. 'I have a meeting in half an hour, I must go. But rest assured this conversation isn't over. I'll try and get back to the hospital before visiting finishes. We'll carry on over dinner.'

'I don't think so,' retorted Lara, chin high, eyes bright.

She'd had enough of this conversation. As far as she was concerned they'd said all that needed to be said.

'You have no choice, dear girl. Not if you want to keep your precious aunt happy.'

Keeping Helen happy didn't mean spending every minute of her spare time with Bryce, decided Lara.

When he didn't turn up again at the hospital she was more than a little pleased. It meant she could have a restful evening on her own. She wouldn't even think about him. She'd watch that TV movie she'd recorded the other day. It would be bliss.

But it wasn't so easy to dismiss Bryce from her mind, especially as the movie wasn't half as good as she'd hoped. In fact it was downright boring, and she was thinking about having an early night when the doorbell rang.

It was nine-thirty and she was in her T-shirt nightie with a smiling bear on the front saying, Hug me. Hardly fitting attire to answer the door. But it rang again loudly and insistently and Lara's thoughts immediately went to her aunt. Although, if she'd taken a turn for the worse, surely someone would have phoned, not called in person. Unless it was Bryce? Maybe he'd been to the hospital and had come to fetch her because... Lara waited no longer. She fled to the door and snatched it open.

'I was beginning to think you weren't going to answer.'

'Is something wrong? Is Helen worse? Is—?'

'Whoa!' he said, holding up his hand. 'There's nothing wrong. I was detained, that's all. Is it too late for dinner?'

CHAPTER NINE

THE moment he spoke Bryce knew it was a stupid question. Lara's answer confirmed it.

'Do I look like I'm ready for dinner?'

He grinned to hide his embarrassment. 'It depends where we eat. If we eat here, it doesn't matter what you're wearing.' He rather liked her in the nightshirt. Hug me, it invited. Dared he? And why was he even thinking such a thing when nothing serious would ever materialise from their contrived relationship.

So why had he come when it was so late? Why bother with her when he knew what she was like? The answer was simple. He couldn't resist her delicious body. And, seeing her in the nightshirt, his thoughts were even more rampant. He wanted to find out whether she was wearing anything underneath. He wanted to touch her softly perfumed skin; he wanted to taste it; he wanted to reacquaint himself with the erotic heat of her.

'It's too late to eat,' she snapped.

Maybe for her! 'Forgive me,' he said, 'but there are some of us mere mortals who have to eat no matter what the hour.' He smiled beguilingly. 'Can't you spare me a crust?'

There was no smile in response. 'Help yourself.' She shrugged. 'You know where everything is.'

'You won't join me? Not even in a drink?' He kept a wicked sparkle in his eyes, not for one minute believing that she was as unaware of him as she was trying to make out. What was it she'd said when he'd accused her of fancying him? That she couldn't help herself because he was good at kissing. Good, was he? Mmm, interesting. He might put that to the test later on. Meanwhile his stomach was growling with hunger.

In the kitchen he found ham and tomatoes and a loaf of bread. It would have to do. He'd have preferred a cooked meal but as Lara was keeping determinedly out of the way he didn't plan on staying in the kitchen long. He loaded the food on a tray, together with a bottle of Helen's wine and two glasses.

He found Lara curled on the couch determinedly watching TV. Her nightshirt was pulled down over her knees, her feet tucked up out of sight, and she ignored him.

'Wine?' he asked, filling the two glasses and holding one out to her.

For a moment it didn't look as though she was going to take it; her eyes shot barbs of resentment and it took an age for her to lift her hand and accept the glass. 'I wish I knew why you're doing this.' She tossed the words grumpily.

'Doing what?'

'Making a nuisance of yourself.'

'I wasn't aware that I was. I thought you—rather enjoyed my company.' Being the type of girl she was she certainly wouldn't have given up on him. She was playing some sort of strategic game, and he'd have to be careful otherwise he might fall into her trap.

No, he wouldn't; what was he thinking? He was the one playing the game. He was going to take advantage. Not

Lara. Not ever Lara. She'd cooked her goose as far as he was concerned.

He sliced the bread and buttered it, laid a piece of ham on top, and took a bite. Out of the corner of his eye he saw Lara watching him. 'Want some?' he asked without looking up.

'I could eat a tiny piece,' she admitted quietly, putting her glass down on the drinks table at her side.

He placed a portion of ham onto another chunk of bread, added a slice of tomato and handed it to her.

'Thank you.'

'You're welcome. I could make some more; there's plenty of ham left.'

'I am rather hungry,' she admitted. 'I forgot to eat.'

Because she'd been thinking of him? Planning? Scheming? He was willing to bet that she wished now that she hadn't been so hasty in turning down his proposal. 'You should have said. Shall I cook us something?'

Lara swiftly shook her head. 'This will do.'

It was a mundane conversation when what he really wanted to do was what it said on her T-shirt. He moved from his chair and sat beside her on the plump, squashy sofa and they shared the bread and the ham, and they drank the wine, and the more she drank the more affable Lara became. But it was all platonic and friendly. And conversely, the more negative signals she sent out, the more he wanted her.

He took the empty plates away but he didn't go back to his own chair. He rejoined her on the couch and she backed into her corner a bit more. 'I—I think it's time you went,' she said huskily.

'You do? Actually I'm quite comfortable here. Helen

and I have sat up many long nights setting the world to rights.'

'But Helen's not here and I am, and I want to go to bed,' she protested.

'Who's stopping you?'

Her eyes glittered warningly. 'You are. You're uninvited and unwanted.'

He wasn't so sure about the unwanted. She wanted to throw him out because he was threatening her sanity, yes. She wanted to ignore him, yes, but she couldn't do it because he disturbed her on a very basic level. He could feel the heat of her skin, almost hear the mad racing of her pulses. What she really wanted was for him to kiss her, quite possibly make love to her. Why else would she have remained so skimpily dressed?

If she really had wanted to keep him at arm's length she would have changed while he was getting his supper. It was an invitation if ever there was one, though he knew she would categorically deny it if he dared suggest such a thing. He didn't stop to think that undressing and dressing wasn't an easy task with her arm still in plaster.

'To go back to our conversation this afternoon,' he said, feeling a sudden need to put the whole situation into perspective, 'I don't believe that you'd have decided you weren't interested, if you'd found out about my true worth.'

Lara lifted a defiant chin. 'Then you're incredibly stupid. I meant every word.'

What a magnificent liar she was. And how desirable she looked in her anger, those magnificent cobalt eyes fiercely flashing, her breasts heaving as she drew in ragged breaths. They were naked beneath the thin cotton, very, very naked, as they had been since Helen had been taken into hospital. They simply begged to be touched.

'And I'm supposed to believe that? A woman with your track record?' He tried to inch towards her without her being aware of it.

'You think what you want to think.' She thrust the words at him furiously. 'My conscience is clear. We all make mistakes; we all do foolish things when we're young. Didn't you ever do anything stupid?'

'Of course I did, but nothing so radical.' Marrying Roger for his money wasn't a mistake; it was a calculated risk. She'd claimed he hadn't treated her well, but he felt himself doubting even that now.

Anger shimmered in Lara's eyes. 'I'm sorry if I haven't come up to your exacting standards. I'm tired of the conversation. Will you please go?'

The angrier she got the more he desired her. He couldn't leave without at least one kiss. He rose slowly to his feet and walked towards the door. 'Aren't you going to show me out?'

It was with reluctance that she uncurled her gorgeous long legs and straightened her nightshirt as she got up. Very decent and proper she was, but it had the opposite effect of what she wanted by exciting him even further.

As she passed by him his hormones whizzed into overdrive and he wanted to grab her and kiss her there and then. Lord, she stimulated him more than any other woman he'd known. He could almost forget what type of a person she was.

He followed her along the hall, his eyes greedy on her swaying hips. He could see the tempting curves of her bottom—and there was no pantie line! His mouth ran dry.

When she reached the door he put his hand over hers to stop her opening it. This was the moment he'd been waiting for, the reasonable excuse. He felt her alarm, heard her sudden indrawn breath, and he turned her gently, oh, so gently to him, hoping that she'd be unable to resist. 'Just a goodbye kiss,' he said as he lowered his mouth over hers.

She did try to pull away; in fact she fought furiously in those first few seconds. But the longer he kissed her the weaker her struggles became, until finally her arms—one complete with plaster cast—came around his neck, her hips pushed against his, and her lips parted in reluctant surrender.

Lara knew it was madness and yet she couldn't help herself. Bryce still had the power to arouse her, even under the most extreme circumstances. She ought to have distanced herself from him the moment he'd arrived. In fact she ought never to have let him in; she might have known something like this would happen.

It puzzled her why he still wanted her. It had to be a sex thing, nothing else. Was it his strange way of punishing her? Taking from her but giving nothing in return? Whatever, there was not much she could do about it. Her mind might war with him but she had no hope of controlling her body.

His hands were low on her back, his mouth hot on hers, his teeth grazing and nipping in an erotic display. She heard the soft moan of her own voice, his groaned response as he pressed her even harder against him.

Bryce's arousal was magnificent; it both excited and shocked her. It made her want to turn around and run, and accept all he had to offer, both at the same time. Though when his hands began to creep beneath the hem of her nightshirt she began to worry. And when his hands cupped her bottom, she knew real fear.

Bryce wanted and Bryce was determined to take. And she wasn't doing a very good job of fighting him off. In fact it must seem to him like total surrender. Could he feel the blood pounding through her veins? The erratic thud of her heart? The surge of excitement in her most private of places? Oh, Lord, how had she got herself into this mess?

Except that it didn't feel like a mess. Maybe later; but for now her senses ruled. Senses urged her to gyrate her hips against his hardness; senses forced her to kiss him more passionately than she'd ever kissed a man before; senses took over every part of her body.

'Oh, Bryce.' The words were torn from her.

In response he slid his hands up to her breasts and she caught her breath as his thumbs grazed her already sensitive nipples. And when he carefully eased her nightie off and teased those same explosive buds with teeth and tongue she mindlessly arched into him.

He took her mouth again, cradling her head with one hand while his other found the hot core of her passion. She was moist and ready and could not have stopped him now had her life depended on it. 'Oh, yes, Bryce, yes,' she whimpered.

With a groan, and without taking his mouth from hers, he lifted Lara in his arms and headed towards her bedroom. She lay moaning softly like a child in pain. She *was* in pain. And only Bryce could make her better.

He kicked open her bedroom door and deposited her on the bed. 'Hold that feeling,' he commanded as he breathlessly ripped off trousers and shirt and shoes and socks, all the time his eyes never leaving hers.

They made love to her, those smoky grey eyes. They tortured her breasts, made the tingling peaks leap out to him; they stroked over the flatness of her stomach until they reached the madly pulsating heart of her. And here they threatened all sorts of pleasures.

She couldn't keep a limb still as her hungry eyes watched him undress. His body was honed to perfection; it was torture to her eyes. She wanted him against her, inside her, filling her. Now! This minute! No waiting!

Bryce clearly felt the same way because his lovemaking was immediate and intense. There was the faint notion that he was punishing her but she shrugged it off, allowed herself to get carried away on a tide of heightened passion, and once the waves of shuddering pleasure had faded Lara felt truly sated. She lay there with her eyes closed, a beatific smile on her lips.

She could feel Bryce beside her, his body hot and sweaty, his breathing gradually returning to normal. He didn't hold her or touch her, as she would have wished; he just lay there on his back, recovering. But she half expected, half hoped, that once he had drawn second breath he would make love to her again.

But the next second he swore loudly and angrily and shot up from the bed. Lara snapped open her eyes and saw him tugging on his clothes, all fingers and thumbs in his haste.

'That was a mistake.' He grated the words out as he yanked up the zip on his trousers. 'A damned big one.'

'I think it's what you had in mind when you came,' Lara said quietly, refusing to let him see how hurt she felt.

There wasn't even an apology. 'It certainly didn't come over you suddenly. The way you were eyeing me all evening made it a foregone conclusion.'

'So why didn't you stop me?' he jeered. 'No, don't answer. There's still hope, isn't there, that I might change my mind? You think that if you let me make love to you, I'll find you irresistible. You think I might ask you again to marry me, and this time you'll jump down my throat in your haste to say yes.'

Furious that this was his interpretation of their lovemaking, Lara pushed herself off the bed, dragging the sheet over her nakedness which had now become an embarrassment, and storming right up to him she glared into his eyes. 'Don't flatter yourself, mister. You were the one who attacked; you were the one who set out to make love to me, so don't try and pass the buck.'

Standing so close that she could smell his sexuality, feel the heat of him still, Lara wanted nothing better than to turn tail and run. But faintheartedness wasn't part of her make-up. She firmed her chin and refused to budge, her eyes unwavering on his.

'It takes two to tango, dear girl,' he pointed out as he shrugged into his shirt.

'I might have known you wouldn't accept any responsibility,' she snapped. 'But let me make it clear right here and now, there will never be a repeat of this performance. If you dare try to even kiss me again, you'll be sorry.'

He looked amused rather than offended by her outburst. 'You're quite the little spitfire when you get going.' He sat down on the edge of the bed to pull on socks and shoes. Lara looked mutinously down at him. And when he got up he said, 'Don't forget, we're still good friends in front of your aunt. Don't dare let me down.'

'I think it will be best,' she said hotly, 'that you don't visit when I'm there. That way there'll be no problems.'

'It won't work,' he said tersely. 'Play the game, Lara, or else.'

'Or else what?' she couldn't help retorting. How dared he think he could threaten her when he was the one doing all the running.

'Or else you'll have me to contend with.'

'If the little scene earlier is any indication of how you intend to keep up appearances,' she retorted, 'forget it.'

'There'll be no repeat,' he assured her. 'I must have been out of my mind.'

'Were you out of your mind when you suggested that we put on a performance for Helen's benefit?'

He shook his head angrily. 'They are two separate things.'

'So exactly why did you come here tonight?'

He didn't answer. He marched to the door and wrenched it open. And contrarily Lara felt sad that the evening had to end like this.

When he had gone she flopped down on the sofa and ran through what had happened. There was no escaping the fact that Bryce had come here with the express intention of making love to her. And fool that she was she had put up no fight. In fact she had enjoyed it totally, except for his anger afterwards. But how dared he blame her. He'd been the instigator; he was the one who'd planned to seduce her; so by what stretch of the imagination could it have been her fault?

It was late when Lara decided to go to bed. She was

tired and out of sorts and it was impossible to sleep. Images of Bryce kept popping into her head: a totally naked Bryce with a fine body that any woman would love to touch; an out of control Bryce reaching his climax, his shuddering body heavy on hers; and the anger afterwards when he laid all the blame on her.

At the hospital the next day Lara had her plaster cast taken off, and to her delight her aunt was also discharged. And amazingly, when Bryce showed up at the house, it was easy to pretend to be friends.

Easy because Bryce made it so. There was no sign that anything had gone wrong, no hint that they'd ravaged each other's bodies and had then fallen out afterwards. He played the part of friend and lover to perfection. Aunt Helen was totally convinced. And Lara could almost believe it, too.

His eyes were on her often in the days that followed, suggesting things he'd like to do to her if they were alone. His hand reached out for hers so frequently that she could almost believe she meant something to him. He was so good at it that, had she not known any differently, Lara would have thought he'd had a change of heart.

When he was sure that Helen was well enough to be left on her own, Bryce suggested taking Lara out. 'About time, too!' exclaimed the older woman. 'I thought you were going to protect me for ever. I was beginning to feel guilty because you never have any time to yourselves.'

'We don't mind sitting with you,' protested Lara.

'But I mind,' retorted Helen. 'You should be having fun. There's nothing you can do for me here; I'm as fit as a fiddle now. In fact I might ring up one of my friends and go out to lunch tomorrow. It's about time I resumed my social life.'

'If you're sure,' said Lara hesitantly. She didn't mind how long it took for Helen to recover. In fact, the longer the better.

'So, Lara, what would you like to do?' he asked. And the way his mouth curved at the corners, the way he looked as though he found the whole situation highly amusing, convinced Lara that he was fully aware of the dilemma he was posing her.

'I'll leave that to you,' she said smartly.

'How about a trip on one of my cruisers?'

'An excellent idea,' said Helen before Lara could answer. 'I wondered when you were going to show Lara what the serious side of your life is all about.'

He ignored her gibe. 'I have a busy day tomorrow, Lara. But we could make it a dinner cruise. I'll pick you up around seven.'

Lara nodded. 'I'll be ready.'

When they were alone her aunt said, 'You don't look too happy. Don't you want to go with Bryce?'

'It's you I'm worried about,' lied Lara quickly. 'I don't like leaving you.'

Helen waved her hand, pooh-poohing the suggestion. 'Lara, I'm fine. I'm back to my old self.'

'If you're sure?' She wanted her aunt to say no; she wanted Helen to beg her to stay and keep her company. Wishful thinking!

Lara wore a vibrant yellow dress, feeling the need for something bright to boost her flagging spirits. She fastened her hair back with a big slide, allowing only a few tendrils to soften her face, and she applied a deep scarlet lipstick rather than her usual pinker shades—all defensive armour against this man who was intent on ruining her life.

When Bryce arrived she met him at the door. An eyebrow quirked as he looked her over but he said nothing, simply escorted her out to his car—not the old black Ford now that he no longer needed to keep up the pretence, but a sleek silver Mercedes.

'Helen's still out with her girlfriend,' she said as he set the car in motion. 'She phoned and told me not to wait. It sounds as though she's having a ball.'

'But she is coming home tonight?'

Lara gave him a sharp glance. Surely he wasn't thinking of a repeat performance? 'Of course,' she answered crisply.

'You're not happy about this, are you, Lara?' He braked hard as a boy raced across the road after his ball. 'You've tried to make yourself look bright and cheerful but it's clearly artificial. If you didn't want to come you should have said.'

'And upset Aunt Helen?' she snapped, disappointed that he'd seen through her.

'She's not at home now,' he said, growling. 'I could take you back.'

'Except that when she does return she'll ask all sorts of questions that I won't be able to answer,' Lara retorted smartly. 'No, Bryce, we'll carry on as planned.'

'I want you to enjoy yourself.'

'Really?' She allowed her disbelief to show. 'You don't care two hoots about my personal feelings. All you want is my body.'

A faint, ironic smile twisted his lips. 'Then, that makes

two of us. I say, why not make the most of a bad situation?'

Lara was horrified. 'You mean become lovers, just for the sheer hell of it? Just because our bodies refuse to accept that it's all over between us?'

'It could be fun.'

'For you maybe.' She spat the words. But it would be torture for her knowing it had no future.

'Are you saying that you didn't enjoy the other night?' They stopped at a set of traffic lights and he turned to face her, but Lara refused to meet his eyes.

She'd lost control and if it hadn't been enjoying herself she didn't know what was. And he knew it. But there was no need for the question.

'Your silence is answer enough.' Bryce smiled his satisfaction.

'Don't think you'll get away with it again,' she said, slamming the words at him. 'I'm going out with you for my aunt's sake and nothing more.'

'So having a good time while you're doing it isn't a priority?'

'Not in the least.'

'A pity.'

'Why's that?' she snapped. In her opinion all they had to do was see each other occasionally. They didn't have to even enjoy themselves. Nothing mattered so long as Helen was satisfied.

'I can't think of anything worse than taking a girl out and having her sit around like a wet blanket all evening.'

Lara's eyes flashed. 'Maybe I'd be better off going back to England.'

'That really would upset your aunt.' The traffic lights

changed and he shot forward so quickly that Lara was propelled back in her seat. 'She's set her heart on us making a go of it.'

'And maybe we would have done if you hadn't jumped to all the wrong conclusions.' She couldn't help retaliating. She was trying valiantly to ignore the strong, sexy, masculine smell of him that assailed her nostrils and threatened to drive her crazy, but it was impossible.

'Were they wrong?' he asked scathingly. 'I don't think so. Nevertheless, I think we should put all that behind us for the next few hours. Going over old ground is pointless.'

Especially when someone as pigheaded as Bryce would never admit that he'd made a mistake, thought Lara bitterly. But he was right: they were heading for disaster the way they were going.

When they boarded the cruiser, Bryce greeted the captain with a slap on the back. There was no boss and employee relationship here, no barriers. They were friends, good friends by the look of it. 'I'd like you to meet Lara,' he said, turning to her. 'Lara, this is Steve Slater; Steve, my girlfriend, Lara.'

Girlfriend! Lara's mouth began to drop open; only by a supreme effort did she manage to close it and smile and shake his offered hand. 'Hello, Steve.' He was slim and good-looking, probably in his mid-forties.

'Girlfriend, eh?' Kindly brown eyes twinkled in surprise. 'About time, Bryce, old man. You've been too long on your own.'

'It's early days,' insisted Lara, trying to laugh. 'Don't get us married off yet.'

'I was wondering why you'd left Gloria to run your business,' said Steve. 'Now I know why. She's a great gal, though, is Gloria. Good at her job and easy on the eye. There was a time when—'

'That will do, Steve,' said Bryce warningly. 'Come on, Lara, let me show you around.'

Lara frowned, wondering if her suspicions where Gloria was concerned were founded. But there was no time to dwell on it because he was introducing her to the crew, all eyeing her with the greatest of interest.

When they were alone Lara hissed, 'Why do you say I'm your girlfriend? It's embarrassing.'

Smoky eyes mocked her. 'Why else would I entertain a beautiful girl?'

'You don't mind that you'll have to explain what happens when I disappear out of your life?'

'That's my problem,' he said with an expressive shrug. 'Let's not dwell on it. Let's concentrate on having a good time.'

The cruiser was larger than Lara had imagined, and very luxurious. The dining room on the deck below looked as though it had been set up for a royal banquet: crisp white damask, sparkling crystal, lustrous silver, deep blue napkins with the Kayman logo embroidered very discreetly in one corner in silver thread.

'Is this normal?' she asked. 'Or special because the boss is dining here tonight?'

Bryce smiled, well pleased. 'It's always like this. We believe in treating our guests as VIPs. We give them their money's worth.'

'It's very lovely.'

'I'm glad you like it.'

'And you have a whole fleet?'

'Several ships, yes.'

He was being modest. And although Lara hated to admit it, the fact that he was an extremely successful business-man didn't seem to have gone to his head. He was a nor-mal, nice guy, with no pretensions.

The evening was actually very successful. She'd prayed they wouldn't be seated at a table alone and they weren't. There were two other couples, all strangers at the begin-ning of the night but feeling as though they'd known each other for ages at the end.

Helen was home when they got back, and Lara, replete with the champagne that Bryce had insisted on ordering, was very mellow and happy. It pleased her aunt to see them so full of high spirits and she couldn't wait for a blow-by-blow account of the whole evening.

The next morning Lara had a stinking headache and felt sick, and Helen laughingly accused her of overindulging, 'Not that it doesn't hurt once in a while,' she said.

But for the next few days she still felt off colour. It had to be something she'd eaten, Lara decided, even though Bryce had assured her that always only the very best food was served.

She said nothing to him when he phoned, and was pleased with his news that he was flying up to Queensland on business.

'I've no idea how long I'll be away,' he said. 'I'm in the throes of extending my business.'

Take as long as you like, thought Lara. It was a big relief. It would give her the breather she needed. Though why he hadn't told her last night she had no idea. Even Helen thought it was strange. But Lara wondered whether it was his way of getting round their difficult situation.

A week later Lara found out why she hadn't been feel-ing well.

CHAPTER TEN

NEVER in her whole life had Lara missed a period. The realisation that she might be pregnant plunged her into deep despair. She and Bryce had only had unprotected sex once—no, twice. But the other night didn't count. It was in the shower when she'd broken her arm that she was thinking of. That never-to-be-forgotten occasion. Even remembering brought heat to her skin. There was something about that first time...

Of one thing she was certain: though, she wouldn't tell Bryce. She'd leave Australia first. Because she knew that he would immediately assume she'd done it deliberately to trap him into marriage. He had that sort of mind.

And he'd destroy her.

Somehow she managed to hide her nausea from Helen. It helped that her aunt was an early morning person and liked to eat her breakfast out of doors. Only once did she come in when Lara wasn't well and Lara managed to convince her that she'd choked on a piece of fruit.

Bryce phoned often enough for Helen to have no suspicions that their love life wasn't running smoothly. Always he asked to speak to Lara. He'd tell her how he was getting on, he'd talk about all sorts of things except their pretend relationship, but at the end of the conversation, without fail, he'd ask her to say that she loved him. 'Say it loud enough for Helen to hear,' he would insist. 'We need to keep her happy.'

Lara felt dreadfully self-conscious. He was enjoying this game but she wasn't, and she would have liked nothing better than to tell him so, but always her aunt was within earshot.

When, one evening, Bryce announced that he would be back the next day she felt swift, heart-pumping alarm. What if he saw there was something wrong with her? What if he guessed about the baby? He looked at her far more closely than Helen ever did. What was she to do?

Be brave and be bold, she told herself. Act as though there's nothing wrong; don't give him the merest hint.

'I don't know what time I'll be there,' he said. 'It could be fairly late. Whatever you do, don't go to bed. It's not the sort of thing an excited girl in love would do.'

Lara wasn't sure whether there was a double meaning here—don't go to bed until I get there. Meaning what? Or was it all in her mind? Was she thinking too much about sex with Bryce, how good it could be, how he managed to arouse her to heights previously undreamed of, how it had resulted in her expecting his baby?

When Bryce did turn up, she had almost decided that he wasn't coming and was indeed thinking about going to bed. Helen had already gone. 'I'm tired,' she'd said, 'I can't wait up any longer. Besides, it's you he wants to see, Lara. Give him a kiss for me.'

This was the last thing Lara intended doing. She wanted no further intimacy with Bryce, not even a modest kiss. She needed to begin the distancing process.

Lara's first thought when she opened the door to Bryce was how tired he looked, and her second that he still looked as sexy as ever despite the lines of fatigue around his eyes and mouth. 'Come in,' she said, surprised to hear how husky her voice sounded. This was all wrong, she didn't want him here so why feel weak at the knees? Why did her heart do a drum roll? 'Helen's gone to bed,' she said abruptly, 'but she sends you her love.'

'It's late, I know,' he said, 'but—'

'You should have left it until tomorrow.'

'I'm your anxious lover, don't forget.' His bluey grey eyes swept over her face, as she had known they would. 'You look worn out. Has Helen been running you ragged?'

Lara gave a weak smile and shook her head, butterflies playing games in her stomach. 'It's past my bed time.' She turned her head away, not wanting him to read any more tell-tale signs. 'Can I make you a drink?'

He groaned and rubbed a hand wearily over his brow. 'A good strong cup of coffee would go down a treat. I know they say it's bad for you late at night but my need has never been greater.'

So why had he insisted on coming? It didn't make sense. Not even her aunt would want him to visit if he was so tired.

She made the coffee and took it out to him on the veranda. She thought he was asleep, his long legs stretched out, thumbs hooked into his belt, his head resting on the back of the chair. But as she approached he looked at her from beneath lazy lids.

Lara was glad it was too dark for him to see the warmth that flooded her cheeks. Over the last few days she'd made every endeavour to shut him out of her mind, convince herself that he didn't mean anything to her any more, but he only had to come within spitting distance and she was virtually his again.

'This is the first moment's peace I've had since I went

away,' he said, seeming to be speaking more to himself than to her.

'Was your trip successful?'

His nostrils flared faintly. 'Is there any particular reason for asking?'

Lara didn't need the intelligence of Einstein to know what he was thinking. But she refused to be drawn. 'None at all. We had a postcard from Charlie yesterday. She's in Coober Pedy.'

He acknowledged her change of subject with a wry lift of a brow. 'Buying up all the opals?'

'She's met this guy there and is deeply in love. So much so that she's found herself a job in one of the opal shops so that she can be near him.'

'That young lady would fancy anything in trousers,' he commented lightly.

Lara nodded.

'In fact,' he said, seeming to find the whole concept highly amusing, 'I think if you hadn't been around she'd have set her sights on me.'

'Did you fancy her?'

'Not on your life.'

And yet he had taken this other girl's word against hers!

Bryce knew it had been a crazy idea coming here, but he'd been driven by demons that constantly plagued him. Whatever else he might think of Lara her body drove him wild. Thoughts of making love to her had tormented him every night he'd been away.

He'd lain awake most nights in his hotel room imagining her next to him, touching her, holding her, entering her. Entering her! Hell, he'd never fantasised like this over any other woman before. And those feelings had driven him here tonight even though it was almost midnight.

The absurd part about it was that he could do nothing to relieve them whilst Helen was in the house. Not that she'd be shocked—Helen was very much a woman of the times—but his own sense of propriety wouldn't let him. It didn't stop his mind running riot though.

The only light on the veranda spilled out from the room behind them and Lara's face, as she sat down beside him, was in shadow, except when she turned his way. Miraculously then, the amber glow from the lamp chased away her tiredness and made her look incredibly sexy.

Everything inside him surged into life. Damn! And damn again! He should keep away; he shouldn't do this to himself.

If it hadn't been for Helen and their long-standing friendship he'd have parted company with Lara long ago. He'd have kicked her out of his life without a second thought. Unhappily, being forced into her company kept his feelings alive. They tortured and tormented; they unhinged his mind, made him unable to concentrate. On several occasions during this last trip his mind had wandered off on a tangent and he'd had to ask people to repeat what they'd said. He'd received some very strange looks.

'Are you listening to me, Bryce?'

He was doing it again! With the very person who was the cause of all his troubles. 'I'm sorry, what did you say?'

'I said, I'm thinking about going back to England very soon.'

He sat up straight; she had his full attention now. 'You can't do that.' Then he metaphorically clapped a hand to his brow. A ridiculous statement when it would be in both their interests, especially his. His life would get back to normal, no more impossibly erotic thoughts, no more sleepless nights.

'Why can't I?' She looked at him coldly and he could almost imagine the hairs on the back of her neck standing up like a cat's when it was ready to fight.

'Because of Helen.' Because he wanted her, dammit! Despite everything, he wanted her. How stupid could a man get?

'Helen will get over it. I'll broach the subject gradually.'

'She'll still be upset. It could trigger another heart attack.' Emotional blackmail! For goodness's sake, he was better off without her. What was wrong with him?

'I said, I'll be careful.' Her lovely blue eyes flashed warningly. 'And I'd appreciate it if you cooled our relationship meantime. I can't have you coming on to me with all guns firing if I'm preparing to run back to England.'

He couldn't help smiling. Is that how she saw him? It was an apt description when he made love to her. She fired him up magnificently.

'I don't think it's funny,' she snapped.

'It's not,' he agreed, straightening his lips. 'But it's impossible.'

'Why?'

'Helen's too astute. We'd need a solid reason for ending our relationship.'

Lara looked away, sipping her coffee, staring out at the twinkling lights the other side of the river. She'd gone very rigid, he noticed, and really he ought to be pleased that she wanted to leave. And he was, he assured himself. It proved that she'd given up on him.

'I'm sure you're clever enough to think of one.' She

tossed the words at him coolly. 'Unless you'd like me to suggest a few defects in your character that I don't like. Is my aunt likely to listen, do you think? Or can you do no wrong in her eyes?'

'Helen knows me as well as my own mother.'

'So it's me who has to be the bad guy.' Lara looked at him, her eyes still flaring magnificently, her lips thin and tight and angry. 'You could tell her you've done your best but you can't forgive or forget.'

'I might do that,' he nodded grimly. 'But not yet. Helen doesn't need any more shocks for the moment. As you say, we'll have to play it slowly.' He picked up his coffee and drained the cup. 'I'll be going.' It had hardly been worth him coming. All he'd done was add to his torment. What had surprised him was Lara's decision to leave. What had brought that on? Was he missing something here? He'd assumed, obviously mistakenly, that she would sooner or later try to engineer another proposal of marriage. He couldn't believe that she'd given up so easily.

He heaved himself to his feet and Lara followed him to the door. This time he didn't attempt to kiss her; he did nothing except give her a tired smile. 'Goodnight, Lara. Tell Helen I'll call her tomorrow.'

Several days went by during which Lara managed to avoid speaking to Bryce whenever he phoned. She went out as much as possible, walking, shopping, hopping on a train into the city.

To begin with Helen assumed Bryce had a lot of work to catch up on, but when a week had passed and he hadn't been to see Lara, nor even invited her out, Helen began to ask questions.

'Have you and Bryce fallen out again?' She wanted to know over supper one evening.

It would be the easiest thing in the world to say yes and be done with it, thought Lara, but already she could see signs of worry in Helen's eyes and so she smiled. 'How could we have done when I haven't seen him? He's just busy. He told me he wouldn't be around much for a while.'

'That's all right, then,' said her aunt. 'It's just that you haven't been looking well lately, and I wondered if—'

Lara stopped her aunt with an upheld hand. 'There's absolutely nothing to worry about, Helen. Really.' But how long would it be before Helen accepted that the union she was hoping for would never take place?

Two days later when Lara was feeling particularly nauseous her aunt walked in from outside, took one look at her pale face and said, 'It's not a piece of fruit this time. You'd better tell me what's wrong.'

Lara swallowed hard and prepared to bluff it out, but her aunt got in before her.

'You're pregnant, aren't you?'

Lara nodded and dropped her head into her hands.

'You poor child.' Helen immediately pulled up a chair to the breakfast table and draped a comforting arm about her niece's shoulder. 'Why on earth didn't you tell me? Does Bryce know? I guess he doesn't, otherwise he wouldn't be able to keep away. He'll be thrilled. He's always wanted children.'

Maybe! But not with her; never with her. 'I don't want him to know,' she said quietly. 'Not yet, at least.' This was going to scupper her plans. Her aunt would never hear of her leaving now.

'But you must, Lara,' she insisted. 'He has every right.

What are you thinking? You don't have to rush into marriage—I know what you young people are like—but Bryce must know. Phone him now, tell him, make him the happiest man in the world.'

'He won't be happy,' muttered Lara, looking up at her aunt with huge, sad eyes. 'You may as well know it; we never did make up; it was all for your benefit.'

Helen stilled for a second and Lara was afraid that she'd said too much too soon. But then her aunt firmed her shoulders. 'So that was your game? I did wonder. There were times when I felt that things weren't quite right. But, regardless of what's gone on, this makes all the difference. I suppose you could say it's the best thing that's happened. Bryce won't be able to resist you now. You'll see; all will be well.' She looked at Lara's worried face. 'You do love him, don't you?'

'I don't know.'

'But of course you do. I've seen it with my own eyes. You were as miserable as sin when you rowed and thought it was all over.'

'That was because I didn't like what he said to me, what he was accusing me of.'

'But surely that all changed when I assured him I hadn't given away his secret?'

Lara shook her head. 'It made no difference. He thinks I'd marry him like a shot because of his money. Actually I want no part of it. I wouldn't marry him if he begged me.'

'You'd spite yourself because of some silly argument?' asked Helen with a shocked frown. 'And how about Bryce? He's in love with you, too, you know. You can't do this to him; it's not fair.'

Lara shook her head. 'You're wrong. Maybe Bryce did love me at one time, but not any more.'

Helen shook her head in desperation. 'What is it they say, there's none so blind as those who don't want to see? Lara, love, take my word for it. He loves you, even if he doesn't know it himself.'

But Lara was adamant about not telling him.

And Helen was equally determined that she should. 'If you don't, then I will.'

Lara gasped. 'You can't! It's my body, and if I don't want Bryce to know it's up to me.'

Helen held up her hands in mock horror. 'OK, you win.' And she smiled tenderly. 'For now.'

But Lara didn't trust her, and deep down she knew that he had the right to know. Running away to England wasn't the answer now that her aunt knew the truth. She ought to have left earlier, the moment she knew that she was pregnant, then no one would have been any the wiser.

As though he'd homed in on their conversation Bryce turned up early that evening. Helen greeted him with a hug and a kiss and then suggested that he take Lara out. 'It's been so long since you've had time alone—unless you'd like me to go? Not that I feel like it; there's a good movie on TV that I want to watch and—'

Bryce laughed. 'Whoa, there. I get the message. Lara, what are we going to do about this interfering friend of mine?'

Lara hid her inner anxiety. 'It looks like we have no choice.'

'Have you eaten?'

'Not yet.'

'Then, dinner it is. You've won, Helen. Don't blame us if you feel lonely.'

In his car Lara felt her anxiety deepen. She knew exactly what Bryce would say when she told him. Perhaps best to wait until the end of the evening. Why spoil a good meal? She'd hardly eaten all day and was now starving.

But when he took her back to his house she felt alarm bells ring. What had he in mind? Another seduction scene? It was time to use her body again? Her fingers curled into her palms, hurting where her nails dug in, but her lip curled derisively. He'd hardly do that when she told him her news.

In fact it was perhaps best that they were going to be on their own; otherwise he might cause a scene. He was unlikely to keep his voice low; half the restaurant would hear.

And when Lara saw a small table in the window alcove of the dining room beautifully set for two it became clear that he'd made his plans carefully. 'Bryce?'

He gave a lazy shrug. 'Courtesy of my housekeeper. Helen's been on at me for days to invite you out.'

'You were lucky we hadn't eaten.'

'It's why I came early.'

'Not because my aunt asked you?' Lara couldn't help wondering whether Helen had phoned Bryce after their conversation this morning.

'Why would she do that?'

'She was questioning why I hadn't seen much of you lately.'

Bryce's brows rose. 'What did you say?'

Lara shrugged. 'That you were too busy.'

'Good guess; I have been. She wasn't getting over-worried, was she?'

'I don't think so.'

'Good. Let's eat, shall we? And you can tell me what you've been doing with yourself these last few days.' He held out her chair and his fingers brushed her shoulders as he made sure she was settled comfortably.

'As if you're really interested,' retorted Lara sharply, attempting to ignore her heightened awareness, the shivers that had run down her backbone. Hell, why did her senses always come into play when Bryce was near? Didn't her body have the wisdom to understand that this was her enemy?

'This is going to be as much of an ordeal for me as for you,' she added warningly. The worst part was how to tell him about the baby. Did she go for the jugular and blurt it straight out? Did she waltz around it, dropping hints? Or did she meekly say she had a confession to make and tell him as apologetically as she could?

'Is that how you see spending time with me these days, an ordeal?' he asked, eyes narrowed on her face.

'It's what you've made it.'

His eyes narrowed at the terseness of her reply. 'I hope you haven't let Helen see how you feel about me?'

Her eyes flashed. 'Helen thinks we're both madly in love.'

'Good girl. What would you like to drink?'

'Cola, thank you.'

He lifted a telling brow. 'I wasn't thinking of a soft drink.'

'It's all I want.'

He shrugged and rang for his housekeeper to bring a

glass. But when Lara refused wine with her meal he wasn't so amenable. 'What's this, afraid I might get you drunk and take advantage?'

'It's not unheard of.' Let him think that for the moment.

The pumpkin soup was delicious, the best she'd tasted since coming out here, and the rack of lamb seasoned with mint and macadamia nuts was out of this world. Lara began to think that she might enjoy her meal after all until Bryce said, 'There's something different about you, Lara. I'm trying to work out what it is.' His head was tilted to one side as he faced her across the table.

Her heart began a painful tattoo. She had hoped to wait until later, much later.

'Is it your hair? It looks silkier, and your skin has an extra bloom.'

So he hadn't noticed that her breasts were already heavier. Perhaps it wasn't noticeable. Perhaps it was all in her imagination. 'I've merely protected myself from the sun.'

'That must be it.' He carried on with his meal but Lara's appetite was quickly diminishing. She felt more and more nervous with every minute that passed.

'Don't you like it?'

'What?' She looked up to find him watching her.

'Is the food not to your liking? I can ask Mrs B to—'

'Please don't,' she cut in swiftly. 'It's not the food, it's me. I'm not particularly hungry. That soup was very filling.'

He knew she was lying; she could see it in his eyes. They were narrowed and calculating and didn't waver an inch.

'What's wrong, Lara? You've been on edge all evening.'

Lara turned her head to look out of the window, at the silver glints on the harbour from an almost full moon, at Bryce's reflection in the glass. He was still studying her, waiting for her answer. Now, she supposed, was as good a time as any; the longer she waited the more difficult it would become.

CHAPTER ELEVEN

LARA'S toes curled and uncurled in her shoes, her finger-nails digging into her palms, her whole body so taut she felt it would snap. She took a deep breath and turned to face Bryce across the table. His eyes were still narrowed and unfathomable, watching, waiting, wondering, questioning. He knew, she thought. He knew she had something of monumental importance to tell him.

'I'm pregnant.' The words came out all by themselves. Defiantly, loudly, and she held her breath, waiting for the inevitable explosion.

But when he spoke his tone was quiet, too quiet! 'You're pregnant?'

'That's what I said.'

'You're having a baby?'

'Yes!'

'My baby?'

'Yes!' She felt her heart quivering, ready to fall from its safe place the moment the bomb went off. She didn't have to wait long.

There was but a moment's silence before he spoke, a moment when the whole world held its breath. And then his voice was loud enough to raise the roof, to raise every roof in a fifty-mile radius, his eyes blazing like lasers, angry splashes of colour firing his cheeks. 'You conniving little witch!'

Lara's head snapped back as though he had struck her.

She actually felt the pain. And her hands flew in the air as though to ward off a violent attacker.

His chair went flying as he bounced to his feet. 'You planned this, you scheming hussy. You knew I'd never ask you to marry me again, not after I knew—'

'Don't flatter yourself,' Lara cut in sharply, furiously. 'I wasn't even going to tell you. Helen made me do it.' She wanted to get up too and lash out at him but her body was temporarily locked.

His eyes narrowed, vicious straight slits in a face made of granite. Powerful hands clamped the edge of the table as he leaned forward, his face pushed up close against hers, so close she could see each and every one of his pores, every individual eyebrow and eyelash, the faint tracery of lines in the whites of his eyes. 'I'm expected to believe that, am I?' he said, sneering. 'You think I don't know you've—?'

'I knew how you'd react.' Lara shook her head impatiently, bravely, her voice dripping scorn. 'I knew you'd think I'd done it deliberately. God, you're so predictable.' She could smell his anger, feel it washing over her like a giant wave.

'And haven't you?' He blasted the question at her, eyes of ice piercing into her skull.

Lord, she wanted out of here. She didn't want to listen to any more of his accusations. He would never accept that she hadn't planned the whole thing, not if she spent the rest of her life trying to convince him. 'Am I that stupid?' She thrust her words fiercely, her lip curling with distaste. 'I want no reminders of a man who condemns rather than listens to the truth.'

She ordered her rigid limbs to move, scraping back her

chair, rising unsteadily to her feet, all the time her blue eyes hot and hostile on his. 'I knew I shouldn't have heeded Helen's advice. I insist that you take me home.'

To her relief he backed away a pace, but not far enough that she didn't still feel the full impact of his raging anger. 'You're living in cloud cuckoo land, lady. I'll take you when I'm good and ready and not a second before.'

Her heart began a rapid slide into her stomach. It looked as if she was in for a rough ride. Not that she hadn't expected it, but where would it end? 'What's the point in me staying?' she insisted. 'You've already made your feelings perfectly clear.'

Eyes that could be so excitingly sexy, but were at this moment blazing like fireballs, locked rigidly into hers. 'There is every reason. There is much to talk about.'

Lara had other ideas. 'I don't think so.' Her chin lifted defiantly, her eyes matched his for blazing determination. 'I'm returning to England; there's nothing you can do about it.'

'Damn you!' He lurched towards her, his hands reaching for her throat, and Lara thought for one terrified moment that he was going to strangle her, put an end to her life, baby and all. But instead they took her head, held it in a vice-like grip, forcing her to look into the flaming depths of his eyes. 'Damn you to a life of torment in hell,' he said, gratingly, his top lip curled upward and outward, his teeth bared like a dingo in danger.

'You're so sweet, Bryce.' How she managed to sound normal, how she managed to inject just the right amount of sarcasm into her voice, Lara didn't know. Not when she could feel his pulsating anger, when his whole body was swaying over her, threatening, scaring… 'But I somehow think that you're the one who's going to end up there.'

His nostrils flared tightly, muscles jerked in his jaw as he fought for control, but gradually his hands relaxed and he took a step back. He dragged in a much needed breath. 'Say what you like, but I will not allow you to leave. We need to talk; we need to come to some—some amicable agreement.'

'Amicable?' She gave a light laugh. 'Is that possible?' And she rubbed her hands over her head where she could still feel the imprint of his hard, punishing fingers. 'Your opinion of me is so low that I'm sure you'd like to grind me beneath your heel, not have me hanging around.'

'We have the baby to think of.'

Lara lifted her brows and waited to hear what he had to say next. Bryce had been predictable in his behaviour so far, but she had no idea how he would suggest they resolve this situation. As far as she was concerned, bringing the baby up on her own was by far the best solution. If she hung around here he would make her life unbearable.

Bryce paced the floor, his tread heavy, his head bowed. He seemed to have aged ten years in the last ten minutes. But Lara didn't feel sorry for him. She watched, saw the moment that he made his decision, saw his back straighten, his feet become still, his burning eyes penetrating hers once again.

'I want you to marry me.'

Lara stopped breathing. Her whole body shut down. Only her mind was alert. This was something she definitely hadn't expected. He couldn't be serious. What was he thinking? How could that help? His feelings would never change. It was a recipe for disaster. It was unfair to bring up a child in a house of hostility.

And when she did remember to breathe again she found that she couldn't speak.

'Did you hear me?' he asked harshly.

She swallowed hard and nodded. 'Yes.' It was a faint yes, a strangled whisper, but he heard and he nodded.

'I'll make the arrangements straight away, and—'

'I can't do it.'

'What do you mean you can't?' He frowned, fury beginning to show again. 'It's the only solution. And the only reason you got pregnant,' he added pointedly.

'You bastard!' Why did everything come down to that? 'You've read me wrong, Bryce Kellerman. Very wrong. It's not what I want at all. I'll never marry you.'

Eyes narrowed, and she could almost hear his mind working. 'Then there is only one other solution,' he said calmly and coldly and calculatingly. 'You hand the baby over to me as soon as it is born.'

Lara felt as though the lifeblood was draining from her body. She reached out to the chair for support. Instead Bryce's strong arm came around her. It almost finished her off. 'Do you know what you're asking?' she whispered hoarsely.

'It's my child.'

'But mine as well,' she insisted, 'and since we can't split it into two then I think you'll find that the law will be on my side.' She felt cold all of a sudden despite the heat of Bryce's body against her. Cold and ill and worried, and desperately anxious to go home to bed.

'So you have no choice but to marry me,' he snarled,

'because I absolutely refuse to give up my own flesh and blood.'

Lara knew that marrying Bryce would make her the happiest girl in the world, but not under these circumstances. Not when he thought the worst of her. Not when he'd condemned her to hell. What sort of marriage would it be?

An unhappy one! A desperately unhappy one!

She'd be locked into a loveless relationship. He'd care only for the child and nothing for her. In his mind she'd want only one thing out of their marriage, and he'd be determined not to give it to her.

'I can't marry you,' she said quietly but firmly.

'Then, the child is mine,' he declared. There was arrogance in every line of his body. In the proud tilt of his head, in the Roman nose, in the carefully hooded eyes. 'No argument. The child comes to me.' It was a statement of fact. He didn't even expect her to contest it any more. He had spoken!

After a short pause, during which Lara remained silent, he added, 'Now I will take you home.'

Lara knew she couldn't go through with it but she was too tired, or too ill, she didn't know which, to argue. She allowed him to help her out to the car, closed her eyes while he drove her home, feeling nothing, not even a flicker of response. She accepted his arm as they mounted the steps to the house, but she disappeared into her bedroom immediately Helen opened the door.

She could hear their muffled voices, knew Helen must think she was all kinds of a fool, but how could Bryce expect her to marry him knowing that his opinion of her was zilch? It didn't augur well for their future happiness; in fact there would be no happiness. All he wanted was the child. She meant nothing to him any more. She was doing the right thing.

Right in not marrying him.

Not right in allowing him to take the baby.

That would never happen.

She had time, though, to decide the best thing to do, the best way to go. Plenty of time, she decided as she kicked off her shoes and lay down on the bed. She needed to make a home for herself somewhere where he'd never find her. She'd have to give it a lot of thought... Her eyes closed and remarkably, in no time at all, she was asleep. She didn't hear Bryce's car start up, nor Helen tiptoe into her room and pull the covers over her.

She was lost in a world of dreams: a dream where she and Bryce were happily married with several children; another one where he was chasing her through a wood after the baby which she held tightly and protectively in her arms; and yet another where Bryce became the baby and was suckling her breast.

She awoke drenched in sweat, and when she sat up she felt desperately dizzy. It took a few minutes for her to swing her legs out of bed and make her way to the bathroom.

And it was here that Helen found her, crumpled but conscious on the floor.

She was bundled back into bed and the doctor sent for. He scolded her for not going to see him when she'd first realised that she was pregnant, but told her there was nothing to be unduly alarmed about, that she simply needed to take extra care during these first three months.

And then Bryce arrived looking all concerned. Lara gave an inward groan, guessing that Helen must have phoned him. 'What's happened? Is the baby all right?' he asked urgently.

The baby! Not herself! Not a word about her well-being. Lara almost wept in despair. He looked as though he had got out of bed in a hurry: his shirt buttoned up wrongly, his hair awry.

'Everything's fine,' she told him. 'Helen panicked for nothing. You don't have to worry.'

'But I do, I am. Are you all right, Lara?'

So here it was, the question he ought to have asked in the beginning. 'Yes, I'm OK.'

'Is there anything I can do for you, get you?'

Lara hid a wry smile. 'Nothing, thank you.'

'Oughtn't you to be in hospital? Oughtn't they to check you out?'

'It was a silly fainting attack, that's all,' she told him impatiently, 'and I'm not even sure it was that. I was giddy and fell over. I'd had a bad night.'

'You need plenty of rest.'

'Maybe, but I don't need you to tell me to do it,' she retorted huffily. 'Thank you for coming; you can go now. I'm sure Helen will keep you informed on my progress.'

But instead he sat down beside the bed. 'Was any of this my fault?' he asked with a worried frown. 'I wasn't the politest of people yesterday.'

Lara shook her head and then wished she hadn't because she still felt light-headed. 'It had nothing to do with you. I had some bad dreams and woke up sweaty and out of sorts. I need a shower actually and then I'll be fine.'

'Let me help you.'

Was that really herself laughing? It sounded like a witch's cackle, hysterical almost. 'You have to be joking.'

He took her hand into his. 'Marry me, Lara; let me look after you.'

'Go to hell!' she snapped, while noticing that he actually sounded as though he cared. It was without a doubt a front for her benefit. It was only their child he was interested in. He'd made that perfectly clear.

'Lara!' admonished Helen, suddenly appearing in the doorway. 'How can you speak to Bryce like that?'

'I think it's time I went,' he said, not waiting for Lara's answer. 'I'll call by later this evening.'

'You needn't bother,' Lara retorted.

Helen raised her eyes to the ceiling. Bryce sighed and shook his head. They both left the room.

Lara climbed out of bed and hurried to the bathroom. She needed to cleanse Bryce out of her system. She stood beneath the pounding jets of the shower, letting it rain down over her shoulders with all its force. How often was he going to pester her? she wondered as she lathered her body. And how long could she put up with it? If he was going to ask her to marry him every time he came then she was better off away from here.

Her mother would be pleased to see her home but that wasn't the answer. She didn't know what it was yet. She didn't even feel that she'd got the energy to start over somewhere else. And what would she live on? She could get a job short-term she supposed, but when she was forced to give that up, what then? What little bit of savings she'd had had been spent in the short time she'd lived here. Helen had said not to worry, but really she couldn't sponge off her aunt the whole time.

She'd made a mess of her life by allowing Bryce her body. He'd never truly loved her or he wouldn't have believed she was capable of getting pregnant for the specific reason of inviting marriage. He'd lusted after her, that was all, and it was a love-hate thing that she felt for him now. She wanted him out of her life but he wasn't going to go away. She was the one who had to do the disappearing act.

But not yet, not until she felt up to it. So long as she did it before the baby was born.

The shock when Lara told him she was pregnant was nothing like Bryce had ever experienced before. It had stunned him with the force of a rubber bullet. How could it have happened? It didn't make sense. He'd always been so careful. And the fact that he'd asked her to marry him made no sense either. It had been a difficult decision; he'd thought hard about it, thought he was doing the decent thing—and yet she'd turned him down!

She was unbelievably hostile, so adamant that she didn't want to be his wife, despite the child they'd made together. He knew he hadn't been kind, but surely the baby made a difference. He couldn't understand it. At least she'd agreed to let him have the baby—or had she? Now he came to think of it she hadn't actually agreed to anything. He had, in his own arrogance, announced that he was going to take the baby. She had said nothing.

He would need to watch her carefully. He didn't want her running away and putting the child out of his reach. Maybe marriage would work. So what if she was interested in the good life? Did it really matter? He could afford it. She was good in bed as well as being good to look at. He could do worse though he'd hoped for so much better. And dammit, he wanted his baby.

He would need to work on Lara, try the softly, softly approach, convince her that he'd had a change of heart, that he wanted to marry her for all the right reasons. He tried to ignore the fact that his heart said they'd always been the right reasons.

But when he called to see her that evening, after a hard day of meetings and difficult decisions, she was as hostile as ever, and he knew it was going to be a long, hard slog to get her round to his way of thinking.

She and Helen were both sitting on the swinging seat on the veranda enjoying the last of the day's warmth. Helen jumped up immediately, pleased to see him, and offered him her seat before leaving them alone together, but when he sat down Lara inched away.

He pretended not to notice. 'How are you?'

'Better.'

'No more dizzy spells?'

'No.'

'That's good. Have you been out today?'

'No.'

He controlled his impatience with difficulty. 'Have you nothing else to say for yourself?'

She turned to him and glared. 'I don't want you here.' The words were loud, resentful and emphatic.

'Now, that's a pity,' he said smoothly, knowing that if he retaliated in similar form it would get him nowhere. 'Because I want to be here. This is our child you're carrying, Lara. I want to be a part of the whole process.'

'You should have thought of that a lot earlier,' she riposted. 'You're not getting a second chance.'

She was hurting, he could see that, really hurting, yet she'd brought it all on herself. And he'd had Charlie to thank for stopping him making a fool of himself. But now things had changed; he wanted her back in his life; he couldn't allow her to take his child away from him. He'd always wanted children, planned to have them still, some day. But in his mind the first-born was always special. Whatever it took he would not allow Lara to deprive him of this pleasure.

'Lara, would it help if I apologised?' He was prepared to do almost anything to get what he wanted.

'For what?' She arched her fine brows and looked at him scornfully. 'For not believing the truth? For making me pregnant? For swearing you'll take my child away from me? Or is it all three you're referring to? Go away, Bryce, I don't want to see you again.'

She was so magnificent in her anger. He shook his head, clamping his lips together, knowing that if he wasn't careful he'd say something that would kill their relationship altogether.

'Look, Lara,' he said at length, 'I know you're hurting; I'm hurting, too. Why don't we call a truce?'

Somewhere at the back of his mind came the niggling thought that perhaps he was doing her an injustice. He had no proof that she'd turned him down because he wasn't in the millionaire bracket to which she aspired. And the fact that she'd scorned his latest proposal must mean that this wasn't a carefully constructed plot either.

Or was it?

The doubts still persisted.

Did she know that he wouldn't rest until he got his own way? Was she banking on this, knowing that it would put her in a better light? He really didn't know what to think any more.

Her eyes flashed hotly at him now. 'We tried that for Helen's sake; it didn't work then, it won't work now. We've gone beyond making up.'

'No, we haven't,' he protested fiercely, his mind still full of conflict. He'd had time to realise how badly he'd reacted to her announcement. It didn't bear thinking that he might have ruined any faint chance he had of marrying Lara and being a proper father to their child.

He still loved her! The realisation came on him suddenly. The emotions he'd thought had died an instant death were still there. He drew in a long, shattered breath. Oh, Lord, what had he done?

'You're in no state to argue,' he told her, his voice deliberately calm now, full of understanding. 'You need to be taken care of.'

'Which I'll get from Helen.'

'The child needs its father.'

Lara gave a troubled laugh. 'I hardly think he'll know at this stage whether you're here or not.'

'He?' He picked up her words sharply.

'A figure of speech. I don't know, and I don't want to know.'

'Lara, maybe I jumped to conclusions. Maybe I—'

She hissed out an angry breath. 'Don't try and get round me that way; it won't work. Nothing you can say will make me change my mind.'

Bryce's heart hung like a lead weight in his chest. He sat there for what seemed like hours, saying nothing; what could he say? Every move he made, she blocked. It needed more careful strategy than he could think of at this moment.

Helen came out carrying a tray with three glasses of her

home-made lemonade. 'I thought liquid refreshment might be in order,' she said cheerfully, pretending not to notice their glum faces.

'I was just leaving,' said Bryce, jumping to his feet.

Helen frowned. 'So soon?'

'Lara's tired.'

Lara confirmed it by nodding. 'I thought I'd have an early night.'

'What gorgeous flowers!' exclaimed Helen, sniffing the huge bouquet of red roses that had just arrived. 'They're for you, Lara.'

Lara frowned. 'Who are they from?' Although, it wasn't difficult to guess. But it wouldn't get him anywhere.

'You'd better read the card.'

'"To the most beautiful mother-to-be, love, Bryce."'

Love! Lara threw the flowers across the room. 'Bin them!' she commanded. How dared he send his love when they both knew his only interest lay in the baby!

'Lara, we can't do that. They must have cost the earth.'

'Then you have them. Put them in your room, I don't want to see them.'

But the next day another bouquet arrived, and every day for a week there were more. The house began to look like a florist's shop because Helen refused to throw any of them away.

And on the seventh day Bryce turned up in person carrying yet another bunch of the despised red roses, one so huge that Lara could hardly see his face.

Helen, naturally, was delighted to see him. Lara simply glared. 'You're wasting your money.'

'I'm trying to make amends.'

'It will take more than flowers.' In fact, nothing would ever erase the hurt in her heart.

Helen took the flowers from him and disappeared; she was very good at melting away whenever he came to see Lara.

'How have you been?' There sounded real concern in Bryce's voice but Lara knew this couldn't be. All he cared about was the baby. Maybe her good health had something to do with it—he'd want her to take care—but she refused to believe that his interest lay in her alone.

'OK,' she answered with an indifferent shrug.

'No more fainting spells?'

'No. Helen's keeping a close eye on me.'

'It should be my job,' he said quietly.

And ruefully, Lara thought, But he'd spoilt any chances he had of looking after her.

'Will you let me take you out?'

Lara frowned. 'I beg your pardon?'

'I'd like you to have lunch with me.'

'Why? You were the one who put an end to our relationship.'

'I made a mistake.'

Ah, yes! And now, because of the baby, he thought he could undo it. Otherwise she wouldn't have stood a chance. He could get lost. 'That's your fault,' she retorted bitterly.

'Please, Lara. Besides, it will do you good to get out.'

'How do you know I haven't been out?'

'I phone Helen every day, didn't she tell you?'

'And was it Helen's idea that you offer me lunch?' she asked tersely. 'I know she'd still like us to get back together. She doesn't hide the fact from me.'

'Helen knew nothing of my intention. Will you come?'

There was something about the way he asked, a sense of humility perhaps, that made Lara hesitate. It would do no harm, she supposed, and she would enjoy a change of scenery. Helen had been very good and had more than once suggested they take a trip out somewhere, but always Lara had refused. She felt so lethargic most days that the effort wasn't worth it. But today she felt much better.

'We could go to the harbour,' he said, seeming to sense that she was weakening. 'You always like it there. We don't have to eat a full, three-course meal if you're not up to it. We could have a snack, or even nothing at all, just sit and look at the water, or stroll. Whatever you feel like doing, Lara.'

He really was going all out to please; it would be churlish to refuse. Reluctantly she inclined her head. 'Very well, I'll come with you.'

And she actually enjoyed the day. Bryce did everything he could to make her happy. It was almost like the first time he'd taken her out. He was the courteous, charming, irresistible, attentive man she'd met and had grown to love.

But the fact remained that he thought the worst of her. And this still rankled. It would for ever more. He could be as nice as he liked; it would change nothing.

He continued to try, however, and Lara kept going out with him, much to Helen's delight. It was as though he was attempting to win her love all over again. Maybe he was, but she had no intention of losing her head this time. She was still quietly thinking about her own plans for disappearing as soon as she found somewhere suitable.

Nevertheless she couldn't ignore the glow that enveloped her whenever he was near, the tingles of excitement that sparked through her veins whenever they brushed against each other, usually accidentally because she was allowing no intimacies. If he had truly loved her he'd have believed in her. This was what she must remember at all times. She must never forget, never let him slide back into her life.

It wasn't easy. The more she saw of Bryce the more deeply she fell in love with him. He was so kind to her, so caring, always concerned about how she felt, how the baby was doing. He made sure she got her daily rest; he made sure she kept her doctor's appointments. He went with her to the hospital for her scan. He involved himself in every way possible. And his interest lay not only in the baby but in herself, too.

If Lara hadn't known differently she would have sworn that he loved her. It poured from him in every way possible. Not that he put it into words, but it was so clear that she could hardly miss it.

What had happened to the belligerence, the arrogance, to the absolute confidence in the belief that she'd set her sights on him for one reason only? She would have liked to think that he'd had a change of heart, but she hardly thought this possible. No matter how convincing he was, it was still an act. All he wanted was the baby.

Her mother phoned one evening when she and Bryce were sitting watching an old black-and-white movie on TV. Helen had gone to a whist drive. 'Why didn't you tell me about the baby, Lara?' were her first words. 'I had to hear about it from Helen, you naughty girl. I didn't even know you had a man in your life. What's his name? What does he do? And how are you?'

'One question at a time, Mum.' Lara laughed. 'I'm ab-

solutely fine. His name is Bryce Kellerman. He's a busi-
nessman, though he seems to have more time off than anyone else I know. He's here with me now—'

'And anxious to speak to you.' Bryce took the phone
off her and began chatting to her mother as though he had
known her all his life, immediately putting her at ease
about Lara, and saying, yes, he hoped to meet her some
day soon. 'How about if I send you a ticket for the next
available flight? I know what mothers are like about their
pregnant daughters,' he said.

Lara fully expected her mother to refuse and was absolutely amazed when she accepted. 'How did you do
that?' she said to Bryce afterwards. 'My mother hates flying.'

'I guess she has good reason to overcome her fear. And
hopefully she'll stay until the wedding.'

CHAPTER TWELVE

INDIGNATION sharpened Lara's voice. 'What wedding would that be?' Bryce had said it with such confidence that it worried her. If he'd already made plans she'd murder him. Or he'd have to carry her kicking and screaming to the altar, and even then she would never say, I do. 'I don't remember saying I'd marry you.'

Bryce smiled easily, confidently. 'But I think you will. I think I've proved over the last few weeks that we're eminently suited.'

'Really?' said Lara, her brows rising. 'What conceit! You've proved nothing. We both know that the baby's the only thing you're interested in.'

To give him his due he looked hurt by her accusation. But she didn't care; it was the truth.

'I can't believe you still think that of me.'

'Why shouldn't I?' she demanded. 'When someone spells out their feelings as loudly and clearly as you did, the message goes very deep.'

'Heavens, Lara, I thought you'd accepted that I said things I didn't mean. I've gone out of my way to prove to you that I do care. Lara—' he took her hands into his '—you and the baby are my whole life. I want you both. Please believe that.'

But he didn't say that he loved her. The words she wanted to hear weren't there. She didn't tug away, but her heart ached. He'd not even attempted to kiss her recently.

A brief peck, yes, when he met or left, but nothing more. Not that she'd have let him, but even so it proved that he didn't love her, still didn't trust her, only wanted his yet unborn child.

And then came the second phone call of the evening. 'Roger!' Lara's voice echoed her dismay, and she saw Bryce grow alert all of a sudden.

She thought for a heart-stopping moment that her mother must have rung and told him her news, but it was nothing like that. 'My court case is next week,' he said plaintively. 'I was hoping you'd changed your mind?'

'Like hell I have,' she riposted, eyes flashing. 'You have no right asking me.' Out of the corner of her eye she saw Bryce frown and get to his feet. She turned her back on him. 'Please don't ask me again because my answer will still be the same.'

'Lara, wait! You can't do this to me. My life will be ruined.'

'You should have thought of that before you committed rape,' she snapped. 'I have no sympathy with you.' And just as Bryce leapt to take the phone from her she slammed it down.

'He's not still asking you to put in a good word for him?' he asked sharply, eyebrows drawn together in a fierce frown. 'If you hadn't told him where to get off, then I most certainly would have done.'

'He's a nasty piece of work,' admitted Lara.

'Exactly how nasty?'

She sat down and slowly shook her head as memories poured back. 'He used to rape me as well.'

'What?' Bryce, who had been on the verge of dropping

into a chair, too, bounced back up on the balls of his feet. He looked ready to spit fire.

'I suppose it's a technicality but it's what it amounted to. He only ever wanted to make love on his terms, when he wanted it, where he wanted it, and to hell with how I felt.'

Bryce swore violently. 'You're well out of it, Lara. I wish you'd told me that before.'

'What difference would it have made?' she asked tiredly. She wanted to forget it.

'Because I'd have gone over there and given him a little of what he deserves. In fact, I think I might still do that. He has no right treating women that way.' He rubbed a hand across his brow, shaking his head, pacing the room.

'It's not worth it, Bryce,' said Lara.

'He needs stopping.'

'I know, but it's none of your business,' she pointed out, more force in her voice now. Goodness she didn't want Bryce fighting her battles; what sort of a girl would that make her feel?

'It is if it affects the girl I'm going to marry,' he declared tersely. 'In fact, the more I think about it the more determined I am to go. The man's a danger to society. Talk about you vouching for his good character; I think what you need to do is stick the boot in. Since you're in no condition to do that, I'll do it for you.'

'No!' Lara jumped to her feet also. 'You can't do that, I won't let you.'

'You can't stop me.'

'Dammit, Bryce, you'll be the one ending up in trouble if you lay a hand on him. He's not worth it.'

'If he keeps pestering you, he's worth it,' he said in a

rasped voice. 'Besides, I can bring your mother back with me.'

Lara shook her head. 'I won't allow you to interfere in my life, Bryce. That part of it is over and done with; I don't want old troubles raked up.'

'Then, lover-boy Roger should keep out of your hair.'

'I agree, but going over there will solve nothing. The courts will decide what to do with him. Just keep away, please.' Still shaking her head she went outside to the veranda. She needed fresh air. She needed space.

When he followed her she turned to him. 'Please, go home.' And she took the steps down to the garden, but in her hurry she missed the last one and pitched helplessly forward.

Bryce's heart filled with horror when he saw Lara trip. He made a futile attempt to save her. She lay in a lifeless bundle at his feet and he was afraid to move her in case she'd broken anything again.

He snatched his mobile from his belt and jabbed in the number of the emergency service. But Lara came round before the ambulance arrived. She looked up at Bryce with a dazed expression. 'What happened?'

'You fell down the steps. The ambulance is on its way.'

'I don't need an ambulance,' she protested, struggling to get up.

Bryce stooped down beside her and laid a gentle hand on her shoulder. 'Stay there, Lara. It's safer. How are you feeling? Does anything hurt?'

'I don't think so,' she said, moving arms and legs experimentally.

'Even so, better to be safe than sorry.' He was worried

about her, the baby too, but Lara more than anything. These last few weeks had been so full of promise. He'd trodden gently and she hadn't rejected him. He'd wanted to kiss and cuddle her, to make love to her even, but he'd been afraid of her reaction. So he'd remained the perfect gentleman, hard though it had been. Now, though, he cradled her in his arms and felt his love flowing into her.

The ambulance arrived in record time. Thankfully Lara had come to no harm but they insisted on taking her to the hospital to check on the baby. Bryce followed behind in his car, dreadfully anxious. He knew he'd blame himself if anything happened to their child. He shouldn't have kept on about her ex but, Lord, he'd been so mad when he'd heard how badly he'd treated Lara. She didn't deserve that; she deserved to be treated like a queen.

His lips twisted wryly at this thought. He'd been as bad as Roger in this respect. They'd both hurt this lovely girl. But never again.

It seemed like hours that he sat in the hospital waiting for news of Lara; in fact it was hours. He paced the corridor; he tried to find out what was going on, all to no avail. Finally the doctor came to see him.

'What's wrong?' Bryce asked urgently. The man looked too serious for it to be good news.

'There's a very real danger that Lara might lose her baby. We're keeping her in. She must have total rest.'

Bryce felt a chill steal through him. In fact more than a chill, he felt as though he'd turned to ice. 'But—she will be all right?'

'Lara will be fine.'

'And the baby?' he asked in a broken whisper.

'All we can do is hope.'

'Can I see her?' Tears were close as Bryce asked the question. For the first time in his life he wanted to sit down and howl. He wanted to beat his chest in anger and frustration. All this was his fault.

'For a few moments.'

When Bryce walked into the ward and saw Lara lying there still and vulnerable, her hair swept back off her face, her cheeks like chalk, it was all he could do to paste a convincing smile on his lips.

'Lara, sweetheart.' He sat beside the bed and took her hand into his. 'I'm so sorry.'

She returned his smile weakly. 'What for? It wasn't your fault.'

He didn't want to argue with her. 'I want you to obey instructions and get better quickly.' He wondered whether they'd told her about the danger to the baby.

'I will,' she whispered.

'Lara, I love you.' But her eyes had closed; she was asleep.

He had no way of knowing whether she'd heard. He'd so wanted her to know; he wanted the knowledge to boost her recovery, to reassure her that she wasn't alone, that she didn't have to bring up the child alone, that he would always be at her side.

'I'll come again in the morning,' he whispered, pressing a gentle kiss to her cheek.

She stirred faintly and smiled. Perhaps she knew.

Bryce had phoned Helen earlier from the hospital, and now he drove back there. She was horrified to hear the news about the baby. 'Lara's sleeping now,' said Bryce. 'There's nothing we can do except hope and pray.'

* * *

Lara couldn't understand what all the fuss was about. She felt fine; why were they forcing her to stay in bed? They said it was because of the baby, but surely they were being overly concerned? It had just been a little fall, for goodness's sake.

Bryce spent hours and hours at her bedside, bringing flowers and chocolates on a daily basis, holding her hand, telling her stories to make her laugh, showing he cared in every way possible. She wanted to ask whether she'd been dreaming when she'd heard him say that he loved her, but was too shy to do so. And he didn't say it again. So perhaps it had been a dream, a wishful dream.

It was almost two weeks before the doctors allowed her home. And she had the most wonderful surprise. Her mother was there. Helen had picked her up from the airport at the same time as Bryce had collected Lara.

It was a tearful reunion. Vera Lennox was openly worried about her daughter, but Lara quickly assured her that all was well now.

During the excitement Bryce had stood in the background. Now Lara held out her hand to him. 'Come and meet my mother. Mum, let me introduce you to Bryce, my baby's father.'

He held out his hand but Vera hugged him instead. 'You look as good as you sounded on the phone. My daughter's a very lucky girl.'

'Perhaps you should tell her that,' he said with a grin.

Later, Helen and Vera, sisters parted for too long, retired to the veranda to reminisce. Bryce and Lara sat on the deep plump sofa in the lounge, half facing but not touching, each curled into their own corner.

After a moment's silence Bryce heaved a sigh and said,

'Maybe this isn't the time or the place, but there's something I need to tell you. I can't wait any longer.'

Lara frowned. It sounded ominous. It had to be about the baby. He was going to insist on taking it from her. He was right: it wasn't the time or the place. She was still far from strong. Goodness, she'd only just got up out of her hospital bed.

Without her being aware of it her hands gripped the edge of the cushioned seat, and she braced herself for what was coming.

'I know I've been a swine to you, Lara. And I wouldn't blame you if you never forgive me. But I've tried over the last few weeks to show you how much I care. Can you guess what I'm trying to say, my darling? I love you. I love you with all my heart.'

Lara didn't move a muscle. She stared at him without blinking. Her throat began to ache, and she swallowed the sudden lump that had lodged there. So it hadn't been a dream! It was what she'd wanted to hear and yet she was afraid, afraid to commit in case something else came along to trigger his distrust. It had happened so easily this time; why wouldn't it again? Could she afford to take the risk? She did love him; of course she loved him. She had never really stopped loving him, but...

'Say something, Lara.'

She had never seen Bryce look so uncomfortable, so unsure of himself. 'I'm flattered.'

'But you still can't forgive me?' He seemed to deflate suddenly, sink back into the corner of the sofa and fade away. Bryce, the man whom she'd always thought so strong and indestructible, was disappearing before her very eyes. He was becoming a shadow of his former self, his skin losing its healthy tan, growing greyer by the second.

'I didn't say that.'

'It's what you think, though.'

'Actually, Bryce—' she allowed herself to smile slowly because her mind was suddenly made up. Life was too short for what ifs '—I love you, too.'

His eyes widened, came back to life. 'You mean that?'

'Yes,' she whispered shyly.

'Oh, Lara.' He closed the space between them in less than a second. Ever mindful of her condition he wrapped her in his arms. His mouth found hers.

Time stood still.

'I've loved you from the moment you broke your arm,' he said eventually. 'From the time we made love in the shower. I went crazy for a little while, but the love never went away; it simply got lost in the red mist of my mind. But I promise you, Lara, it will never happen again. I'll love you for ever; I'll never doubt you.'

Lara's smile was like that of the Madonna. 'That was the time we made our baby.'

He frowned, clearly not believing her. 'I always took precautions.'

'Not that first time,' she said her smile deepening. 'We were both far too impatient.'

Bryce groaned. 'I remember it now. Oh, Lord! When I think what I almost lost it turns my blood cold.'

'You'll never accuse me of wanting you for your riches again?' she asked archly.

'*No!* Never!' He touched a trembling finger to her lips. Lara greedily sucked it in, and when Helen and Vera popped their heads round the door a few minutes later, neither of them noticed.

The wedding ceremony took place at Bryce's house. The bride looked stunning in yards of white lace, the groom extremely handsome in an ivory tuxedo, and the bride's mother cried buckets of tears. The groom's mother, over from New Zealand especially for the occasion, looked emotional as well.

Their guests all exclaimed what a beautiful couple they made, and a lady in her fifties, dressed in lilac silk, with a beautifully deep husky voice told Lara that she was a clever girl capturing Bryce. 'Many others before you have tried and failed. You must have some very special qualities.'

Bryce appeared at Lara's side and nuzzled her behind her ear, his arm possessively about her waist. 'What's the glorious Gloria been telling you about me?'

'*You* are Gloria?' asked Lara, her jaw dropping.

'Didn't Bryce tell you about me?' asked the woman in open delight.

'Oh, yes,' answered Lara, 'but I gained the impression that you were much younger—and, to tell you the truth, I was very jealous.'

Gloria laughed. 'Typical Bryce.'

Bryce turned to Lara. 'You never said.'

'There are some things a girl keeps to herself,' she said primly.

They honeymooned on Hamilton Island in the Whitsundays, and on their return Lara moved into Bryce's mansion built on the hillside overlooking magnificent Sydney Harbour. It was something she'd always said she wouldn't do, marry another millionaire. But this one was different. Bryce Kellerman might be a millionaire, but he was also a man in a million.

Lara knew that she was going to be very, very happy for the rest of her life. He'd promised her that. And she believed him. And when other babies came along they'd fill this house with love and laughter such as it had never seen before. No longer would it seem too big and too empty. Every corner would be used.

Nevertheless Lara still had a soft spot for the boathouse, and many a day when Bryce was out at work she could be found there, sitting watching the boats on the harbour, singing softly to herself and the baby who was growing so quickly inside her.

Bryce's baby. Her baby. She would never have let him take it from her, even if it had meant marrying him without love.

But love him she did, and he truly loved her. Not a day went by without him telling her, sometimes not an hour. His money meant nothing to her. Their life was rich in love, and this was the most important thing of all.

Modern Romance™
...seduction and
passion guaranteed

Tender Romance™
...love affairs that
last a lifetime

Sensual Romance™
...sassy, sexy and
seductive

Blaze™
...sultry days and
steamy nights

Medical Romance™
...medical drama on
the pulse

Historical Romance™
...rich, vivid and
passionate

29 new titles every month.

*With all kinds of Romance for
every kind of mood...*

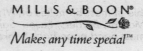

MILLS & BOON®

Makes any time special™

MAT4

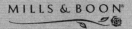

MILLS & BOON
F REIGN
AFFAIRS
A captivating 12 book collection of
sun-kissed seductions.
Enjoy romance around the world
DON'T MISS BOOK 4
outback husbands–
The fiery heart of Australia
Available from 4th January
Available at most branches of WH Smith,
Tesco, Martins, Borders, Eason, Sainsbury's
and most good paperback bookshops.
FA/RTL/4

FREE

2 BOOKS
AND A SURPRISE GIFT!

We would like to take this opportunity to thank you for reading this Mills & Boon® book by offering you the chance to take TWO more specially selected titles from the Modern Romance™ series absolutely FREE! We're also making this offer to introduce you to the benefits of the Reader Service™—

★ FREE home delivery
★ FREE gifts and competitions
★ FREE monthly Newsletter
★ Exclusive Reader Service discount
★ Books available before they're in the shops

Accepting these FREE books and gift places you under no obligation to buy; you may cancel at any time, even after receiving your free shipment. Simply complete your details below and return the entire page to the address below. **You don't even need a stamp!**

YES! Please send me 2 free Modern Romance™ books and a surprise gift. I understand that unless you hear from me, I will receive 4 superb new titles every month for just £2.49 each, postage and packing free. I am under no obligation to purchase any books and may cancel my subscription at any time. The free books and gift will be mine to keep in any case.

P1ZEC

Ms/Mrs/Miss/Mr ....Initials ....
BLOCK CAPITALS PLEASE

Surname ....

Address ....

....

....Postcode ....

Send this whole page to:
UK: FREEPOST CN81, Croydon, CR9 3WZ
EIRE: PO Box 4546, Kilcock, County Kildare (stamp required)

Offer valid in UK and Eire only and not available to current Reader Service subscribers to this series. We reserve the right to refuse an application and applicants must be aged 18 years or over. Only one application per household. Terms and prices subject to change without notice. Offer expires 30th June 2002. As a result of this application, you may receive offers from other carefully selected companies. If you would prefer not to share in this opportunity please write to The Data Manager at the address above.

Mills & Boon® is a registered trademark owned by Harlequin Mills & Boon Limited.
Modern Romance™ is being used as a trademark.